Horizon Alpha Series
Predators of Eden
Transport Seventeen
"High Wire"

Super Dungeon Explore Series
The King's Summons
The Forgotten King
The Glauerdoom Moor
The Dungeons of Arcadia
The Midnight Queen

HORIZON
HOMECOMING
ALPHA

D.W. VOGEL

Future House Publishing

Homecoming

Future House Publishing

ISBN: 978-1-944452-92-6

Cover image adaptation by Brad Duke
Developmental editing by Emma Hoggan
Line editing by Stephanie Cullen
Copy editing by Isabelle Tatum
Interior design by Emma Hoggan and McKenna Limb

Fly free, Josh Vogel

CHAPTER 1

CAPTAIN'S PERSONAL JOURNAL. YEAR ONE, DAY ONE.

I have failed.

I am Theodore Wilde, fourteenth captain of the Horizon Alpha. Thirteen captains before me all performed their duties. They got us here across light-years of space. The planet is exactly as we hoped, with breathable air and a reasonable climate.

The sequence was planned before Horizon left Earth's orbit. We send the first probes and wait for their data. We launch the satellites. We send the Horizon Alpha Away Team for first recon. Once they find a good place to land, we load up the transports and shuttles and head for the surface. The transports were not designed to leave the planet, but the shuttles were supposed to be exactly that, shuttling the rest of our personnel and equipment from the Horizon once a safe colony is established.

None of that is going to happen now.

The probe did its job. But the satellites didn't launch properly. After two hundred years in space, the sensor that should have told me one of the satellites was lodged in the launch tube didn't work. When the next one was loaded and fired, it crashed into the obstruction and caused the explosion.

Things went south quickly. We evacuated the burning ship, everyone scrambling to get into a transport. No orderly lines, no careful packing. Just people screaming and crowding into the little ships while the Horizon burned. Fire doors slammed shut and alarms blared.

We got almost everyone off. That should have been a relief. But the planet's gravity is stronger than we anticipated. Our transports got scattered across a continent, and only half of them landed safely. Several of them seem to be together in a clearing, which might help them survive, but the rest are alone, kilometers away from help. And without the satellites, they'll probably never find each other.

Eighteen of us were left here on the Horizon. The fire system eventually got the blaze controlled, but the ship is a shambles. Of three spinning cylinders, only one is still rotating. The rest are dead and still. The bridge and communications system were devastated, and at the moment we have no way to contact our colonists on the planet. Bethany is working on establishing some kind of communication, but we're down to basic life support. It will take some time. And it hardly matters. Even the smallest shuttles won't be able to get high enough to escape into orbit. No one is coming for us.

We can see the beacons of the transports that didn't crash. We have a rough idea of who was on each one. My wife and sons and my baby daughter were with the largest group. They have the best chance. If the planet is hospitable, they just might survive.

We're all that's left of the human race. It was my job to deliver us all safely to Tau Ceti e, to start a new colony where we could thrive.

I failed. It's right that I should spend my final days on this dead ship, huddling in darkness. It's not right that others are stuck here with me.

Randa, Josh, Caleb, and baby Malia . . . I love you. I'm so, so sorry.

CHAPTER 2

CALEB

The Painted Hall was in chaos. Everybody was talking at once and nobody could hear anything. Mayor Borin waited patiently, sitting in his wheeled chair at the front of the great cavern. Eventually the noise lowered to a murmur as people realized they weren't going to learn anything by shouting questions all at once. They all turned to our elected leader and sat back down, the normal politeness of our society reasserting itself.

Mayor Borin held up his hands for silence. "Communication with the Horizon's remaining crew is a very slow process, but here's what we've learned so far. Twelve people are still alive on the ship in orbit."

The crowd buzzed again, but more quietly and for a shorter time.

"We don't have all the names yet, but Captain Wilde is among the survivors."

I had already told Mom last night when we first made contact with the Horizon Alpha mothership. She sat next to me on the bench along the side wall under the old paintings done by a long-gone alien race. My brother Josh sat on the other side of her, and my little sister Malia was squeezed between us. Mom held the baby on her lap. Now, even though she already knew he was alive, she jumped at the mention of my dad's name. These past three years we had been sure he was dead, left alone on the Horizon. All that time he'd been up there listening to us on our sat trans when the Horizon was in the right place in the sky. He'd heard it all, from our first realization that this scatting planet was full of dinosaurs, to the panic when we were down to our last power core in the early days of electrified fencing around our downed shuttles. He'd listened as my mission fell apart, and when General Carthage died.

I looked down at my half-brother, tiny and perfect in Mom's arms. He was the General's son, named Teddy after my dad. My dad who wasn't dead after all. What must Mom be feeling about that?

The mayor spoke again. "We'll be compiling a list next time Horizon comes into satellite contact. We are communicating by Morse Code, as they are unable to transmit, only interrupt our signal."

On the floor in front of us, my cousin Ryenne sat with her twin brother, Rogan. No one else would ever have understood the message from Horizon, the rhythmic interruption of our trans communication that was their only hope of reaching us. No one but Rogan would ever have realized. But his brain didn't work like other people's. He heard the pattern that was invisible to anyone else. And now there were twelve people alive in orbit around our planet who had been given up for dead three years ago. Twelve people we had no possible way to rescue.

Mrs. Yee stood up in front of the hall. "So we're just going to sit here and do nothing while they die up there?" Murmurs around the room echoed her sentiment.

Mayor Borin shook his head. "At this moment we have no way to mount a rescue. At the close of this meeting I'll be consulting with the council. Horizon should be in range, and our first priority is finding out the identities of our loved ones who are still alive."

The council. That had been a surprise. In the weeks since we returned to Carthage Valley with the survivors of Transport Seventeen, the mayor had put together a group of advisors to help him govern our little community. The idea that we were actually safe enough here to start thinking about our need for government still shocked me. I'd spent too much time out in the jungle to ever feel truly safe again. And the bigger shock came when Mayor Borin asked me to join the council. I was the youngest member, but he said there was no one more qualified than me when it came to surviving outside the valley. Of course, we thought there was no reason we'd ever leave the safety of the valley again.

"There's a shuttle sitting outside the mountains." Don Rand was speaking now, one of the Seventeen survivors. He'd been a pill on the long journey back here, but he was no fool. "I saw the thing when we came in here. Can't we find a way to fix it and go up to get them?"

"I wish it were possible." The mayor nodded. "We salvaged a lot of parts from that shuttle to repair the one we sent to rescue you."

The one that was crushed, its wings torn off, probably by those weird dinosaurs that ran into things with their chests. I shuddered at the memory. They could put a dent into the hull of our largest transport, but they were no match for Titanoboa. The huge snake had made short work of them.

Mayor Borin continued, "Besides, even if it were working, we've never been able to figure out how to get a shuttle high enough to get back into orbit. Right now there is no rescue plan."

The room erupted again, and the mayor gestured for quiet. "We'll keep you informed as information becomes available. For now, we just need to continue what we're doing here. Thank you all."

Everyone stood up, chattering in the echoing cavern. Baby Teddy fussed in Mom's arms.

"Caleb," Mom said, "do you think I can . . ." She trailed off.

I knew what she wanted. "I'll ask the mayor. Dad can hear us talking but he can't talk back. I'll ask if you can maybe come and talk to him after we get the list of names tonight."

She hoisted the infant up onto her chest, cradling his head against her shoulder and bouncing gently from foot to foot. "Thanks." She glanced down at the baby, eyes full of uncertainty.

"He knows about the baby. He knew all along, everything we were doing. He's just happy we're all alive."

Malia wrapped her arms around my leg. She was clingy with me since the baby was born. Or maybe it was just since I got back from the last journey. How many times had she been told I wasn't coming home? Malia would have no memory of our dad.

She looked at me with wide eyes. "Are we gonna fly in the sky?"

I shook my head. "I don't think so, sweet girl. We can't really fly anymore."

"But . . ." Her tongue stuck out one corner of her mouth as she concentrated. "But there's people in the sky?"

She weighed so little as I swept her up into my arms. "There are. But I think"—I shared a look with Mom—"I think they're going to have to stay there."

The Horizon wouldn't be back into satellite contact until late in the evening. Even though I'd been up most of the night, the news that my father and eleven other people were still alive on the ship kept me far too jazzed up to sleep. Everyone was buzzing with the news and the constant questions drove me outside into the valley. I was off pterosaur guard duty today, and had nothing to do with the hours of daylight until we reconnected with my dad in orbit.

No one was quite sure what to do with me. Before the mission to rescue the survivors of Seventeen, I'd been in the early stages of learning to fly the shuttle. We were just getting settled in the valley, figuring out what kind of training we needed to pass on. The remaining adults had all grown up on a giant spaceship hurtling toward Tau Ceti e. Now we were farmers and sheepherders. All the data from Horizon was at our fingertips—how to shear sheep, how to weave cloth from the wool. How to plant the seeds we'd brought from Earth and tend them to feed our growing population. There seemed no need for the advanced nuclear scientists to take apprentices. We weren't going back into space. The medical skills my mom had learned on Horizon were dependent on the technology we'd brought with us. When we ran out of antibiotics and medications, what would we do? Sara and her science team were studying every plant and animal they could grab on this planet, but I was never a science kid. Since the day we landed and saw the 'saurs, all I'd ever wanted to be was a soldier, protecting the little colony from the dangers of the jungle. Now those dangers were a mountain away.

Soon I'd have to make a decision and join one of the advanced training teams. Mom wanted me to become a doctor like her. As I emerged from the shelter of the cave into the bright late-morning sunlight of the plateau that led down into our valley, I glanced up at the cloudless blue sky. I wanted to fly. Now I was grounded forever.

I trooped down the carved stone stairs onto the valley floor. People working in the fields and orchards waved to me as I strolled past, heading for the little wooden barn with the staked wire corral.

"Hey Ryenne," I called as I approached.

She was sitting in the middle of the corral watching her two pet 'saurs devour a pile of cardinalfruit. Their little heads dove into the soft, red fist-sized fruits and came up with their green faces smeared with juice, smacking happily and making the little contented whirring noise they always made when Ryenne was around.

"Hey, Caleb." She held a little carved tube of wood in her lap.

"What've you got there?" I pointed to the tube.

Her face flushed and she tried to hide it in the pocket of her shirt. "It's nothing."

I plopped down beside her and leaned back in the grass,

careful to check for 'saur scat. "What is it?"

One of the 'saurs—Sparkle or Princess, I could never tell them apart—gave a loud burp and waddled over to Ryenne. It tried to shove itself onto her lap but the 'saurs had grown a lot since Ryenne had found them as brand new hatchlings in the jungle. They had imprinted on her and nothing on Ceti would ever convince them that Ryenne wasn't their mother.

She wrapped an arm around the 'saur and it nestled in next to her. Sitting on the ground, her head wasn't much taller than the 'saur's when it stood up. "It's nothing," she repeated, but pulled the little tube out of her pocket. "It's just . . . kind of a flute thing."

I held out a hand and she passed it over to me. Hand-carved from the thick, hollow reeds that lined the lake in the middle of our valley, it had been lovingly polished to a shiny smoothness. "It's really pretty. Did you make it?"

Ryenne shook her head and took the flute back. "Mrs. Desai is teaching music now. I'm way behind on my school stuff, but I think I'm really getting the hang of it. Wanna hear?"

The other 'saur finished off the fruit and waddled over next to Ryenne.

I nodded. "Let's hear a tune."

She raised the flute to her lips and blew into one end. It made a high-pitched whistle, shrill and piercing. Both of the little 'saurs jumped up away from Ryenne and bolted into their little wooden barn, hissing and heads low.

"Wow, it wasn't that bad." I laughed until I saw Ryenne's face. "Aw, it was nice. 'Saurs don't know anything about good music."

She stuffed the flute back into her pocket and stood up, brushing dirt off her legs. "Apparently not." She met my eyes, glared for a moment, then burst out laughing. "Well, maybe I need a few more lessons."

I turned my face to the sun and smiled. "You gotta cut them some slack. Nothing like that's ever been heard on this planet before. They have no history of music appreciation."

"Actually that's not true." Ryenne picked up a little wooden rake and began to clean up the remains of the 'saurs' breakfast.

"There's paintings all over the lower caverns of the birdmen singing. At least, Sara thinks they're singing. She thinks maybe they had some kind of music rituals or something. Singing to the moon. That's what the paintings look like."

I rolled onto my feet and kicked a stray fruit over to Ryenne's pile. "Shame they're not still here. You could form a band. 'Ryenne and the Birdmen.' Go on tour all over Ceti."

She glared at me. "Don't make fun. I'm doing the best I can here."

It wasn't easy. All the adults looked out for my cousins, and Mom had taken over their official guardianship since they had no other family here in Carthage. But we were all family, really. The Seventeen survivors had been trapped in their transport for the last three years. They had a lot to catch up on.

"Where's Rogan?" I asked.

"He's sleeping. You guys kept him up half the night listening to Morse Code."

The little 'saurs peeked out of the open barn door. Ryenne turned and showed them her empty hands. "It's all right, babies. Mama's not blowing the nasty flute anymore. You're fine."

I chuckled. *Mama.* Ryenne's little 'saurs were our distant early warning system for pterosaur attacks, the only dinosaur that still posed a threat to us in our safe little valley. If she wanted to call herself their Mama, no one in Carthage would bat an eye.

"We'll need him again tonight. He's the best at hearing the code and there's so much we need to know. Like, who's even up there? Besides my dad, I mean."

She nodded. "I know. And it's so good for him to have this job. Makes everybody realize he's more than just the weird kid with the hose who doesn't talk much." She looked up, turning her face into the breeze. "I don't know what to hope for. Maybe our mom is up there. Would that be great or horrible? I mean, there's no way we can get to them. So is it better if I know she's up there stranded or if I never find out what happened to her?"

I didn't know what to say. She looked at me with despair in her eyes and stumbled into the little barn to be with her babies.

CHAPTER 3

CAPTAIN'S PERSONAL JOURNAL. YEAR 1, DAY 10

We have completed our preliminary inspection of the remains of the great ark Horizon Alpha. What we have found is not encouraging.

Our ship was constructed with three huge cylinders: fore, midship, and aft, spinning around a central axis. For two hundred years our artificial gravity has been produced by that centrifugal force. We have always been adept at working in zero gravity because the central axis does not spin. It houses the ship's propulsion system, a complex arrangement of nuclear fusion reactors, fuel rods, and power cores that keep the ship running. We also have extensive solar arrays on the outside edges of each of our cylinders.

Each cylinder was designed to be independent of the rest, in case of malfunction. Life support is redundant from one to the next. The explosion and resulting fire destroyed almost all of Tube One, the aftmost cylinder. Unfortunately, Tube One housed our bridge and all the communications equipment. The machine shop where we might have repaired or replaced some of those systems was housed in Tube Two.

Tube Two no longer rotates but was largely spared the effects of the fire. With the machine shop there, we might have been able to re-establish contact with our transports on the planet's surface. Unfortunately, when the explosion occurred and the evacuation started, one of the food service personnel left the solar cover off one of the huge vats of blue-green algae that are our staple food source. When the tube stopped rotating, ten thousand liters of slime were freed to float in zero gravity. Particles of algae are everywhere, spread by the final slow turn of the cylinder as its spin ground to a halt. We may eventually be able to salvage something from Tube Two, but at this moment, it is not a priority.

Eighteen of us are alive in Tube Three. We have gravity, at least for the moment. We have our own algae farm, carbon dioxide scrubbing system, waste management, and water reclamation. As long as nothing else breaks, there is no reason we cannot survive here for years.

But our hope is gone. For generations our ancestors endured their lives on this ship knowing that one day their descendants would walk on a new planet. They knew the profound purpose of their lives: to continue the human race and find a new home for those who would come after them. No one is coming after us. Our people have made it to the planet's surface, and the little we can discern tells us that at least some of them have survived. We cannot hear their voices or see the images they must be recording on the green world below us. They are Ceti-bound, unable to return for us even if they knew we were alive.

So now we wait to die.

None of us has said this aloud, of course. We have kept busy with inspections, salvaging what we can from the damaged areas of our ship. Bethany believes she can rig our communications so that we can at least hear what our loved ones are saying when they use their sat trans on the surface. And we will continue to keep busy with maintenance of our life support here. We pretend there is a purpose for this. That if we can survive long enough, establish contact with the surface, they will find a way to come rescue us.

That isn't going to happen.

This enormous spinning tube will be our coffin. One by one we will perish here until a solitary soul is left alive. Who will it be? What will they think as they walk these empty, desolate halls? How long before our last survivor goes completely insane, and what will they do when that happens? Open the airlocks and pop into cold, empty space? Drown themselves in a vat of algae? Or just sit in darkness, waiting for their own end to come, leaving Horizon Alpha as a ghost ship, a useless, eternal reminder of the failure of Captain Theodore Wilde?

CHAPTER 4

CALEB

Late that night, the Horizon stayed in range for almost four hours. Sara and Shiro sat next to me in Mayor Borin's office. Along with the mayor, there were seven of us hunched over a sat trans, transfixed as Rogan called out the letters he heard in the interrupted hiss of the open line.

"B-E-T-H-A-N-Y-R-A-N-D."

Bethany Rand. Don's daughter. I turned to look at him and saw the knowledge hit him like a Wolf into the fence, all sparks and noise.

"Bethany? My Beth's up there?" He jumped up, wild-eyed. "She's up there?" Before we could stop him, he grabbed Rogan by the shoulders. "Did they say it was Bethany?"

Rogan's hands twisted the soft length of tubing he had carried with him from the Transport. It was always with him, and the more stressed he got, the more he worked that tube in his hands. It was falling apart as he wrung it.

I pulled Don off, scowling at him. "You can't touch Rogan.

He doesn't like it."

"Doesn't like it?" He turned on me. "My daughter is up there! My daughter! And he doesn't like it?"

Adam, who was with me the whole way back from Transport Seventeen, crouched next to Rogan, who was muttering under his breath, twisting the hose in his hands. "It's all right, buddy. Just listen to the letters, okay? What are the letters?"

I gripped Don's arm. "We all have people up there. And right now there's nothing we can do about it, so just sit down and let Rogan hear."

Tears formed in Don's eyes. "She's alive," he whispered.

My heart softened. The man was a colossal pain, a selfish boor. But I knew exactly how he felt.

Rogan resumed calling out letters and soon we had the list. Don's daughter was alive up there, along with my father. Sara's brother-in-law. And Marci, Rogan and Ryenne's mother. *Should have known she wouldn't leave without her kids.* She couldn't have known her young twins had been rushed onto a transport without her. I couldn't imagine how Ryenne was going to take the news. Rogan didn't react, just kept spelling out letter after letter, each one a person we'd thought long dead.

When we had the final list, Mayor Borin spoke to all of us—those in the room with him and those orbiting kilometers above the planet's surface. "All right. We'll let everyone know, and tomorrow when you're in range, we'll get whatever family members that are here in Carthage to come in turns. They'll all want a chance to talk to you, I'm sure."

It would be painstaking, and painful. What did you say to someone you thought was dead for three long years? *I guess you start with I love you.*

"Now," the mayor continued. "Does anybody have any ideas how we can get them down here?"

We'd established that there were no more transports or shuttles on Horizon. No way for them to leave the ship without our help. And at this moment, no way for us to reach them.

"Nirah could do it."

We all turned to stare at Don.

"Nirah could fix our shuttle. She could find a way to fly it."

Mayor Borin smiled. "If anyone could, Nirah could," he agreed. He explained for the rest of us. "Nirah Saffar was Chief Engineer on Horizon. My boss"—he nodded at Don—"and Don's boss. She could cobble together just about anything, and it's a good thing, too. Those last few years before we got here, well . . ." He sighed. "Without Nirah, I doubt we'd have made it here at all."

Rogan grunted and we all hushed to listen.

"N-I-R-A-H-T-R-A-N-S-0-8."

"Transport Eight?" Mayor Borin spoke into the trans. "Nirah was on Transport Eight?"

Rogan listened to the hiss and said, "Y."

Yes. But what good would that do us?

It took most of the time we had left, but by the time the Horizon drifted out of our range, we had learned several more things. They had beacon signals from all the ships that didn't crash. They knew which transport Nirah was on. They knew where it had landed. They knew that at least some of the people on that transport had survived the flight. The ship was at the far northern limit of Horizon's satellite range, and they could only hear their sat trans signals for a couple of days each summer. But as of five months ago, some of them were still alive.

"Is Nirah one of them?" Don shouted into the trans.

Rogan shook his head and twisted his hose. The hiss of the open trans line was unbroken. Horizon had gone out of our range for the night.

We pulled up the map with the coordinates for Transport Eight. It was about twenty kilometers northwest of us, straight up through the mountains. And . . .

"Oh, scat," I muttered. "Is that a river?"

The picture focused in, and Sara squinted at the image. "It looks like a sea channel. A river is made up of little streams that flow down out of the hills, all running together. A sea channel is salt water. Ocean. It's cutting through right here." She pointed at the image where the land narrowed. Dark water cut across the map like a belt across the jagged mountains. "It comes from here." She pointed to a large body of water surrounded by mountains. "The channel connects this body of water to the ocean. Probably too salty for anything to live in that inland sea, but that won't help us. And the channel here is not very wide."

"Too wide for the tree trick?" I glanced at Don.

He shook his head. "No way. This is almost as wide as our whole valley. No way we can bridge it."

"Is there no way around it?" I widened the view, looking at the distance around the inland sea that divided our mountain range from the one where Transport Eight had gone down. The channel was by far the narrowest point for us to cross. It would take months of mountain climbing to trek all the way around the north edge of that water.

Mayor Borin frowned. "Those are real mountains up there. We're in the foothills. Elevations there look more than twice as high as ours. We don't have the equipment or expertise to get anybody around that way."

Sara chewed on her lip for a moment. "There are zodiacs in storage?"

It had seemed stupid to bring the little inflatable watercraft from our original landing site, but we'd brought everything we possibly could when we made the move from the fenced ring of downed transports. No way we were going to use them on the water here. Very bad things lived in the water of Ceti. But the zodiacs were good solid rubber.

"If nobody has cut them up to make something else, I think there were three of them," Mayor Borin said.

Sara nodded to herself. She looked at me and pressed her lips together. "I have an idea to get across that channel."

Every eye stared at her.

"I think," she said, "it's time we started to train the dinosaurs."

CHAPTER 5

CAPTAIN'S PERSONAL JOURNAL. YEAR 1, DAY 42.

Bethany fixed the ship-to-planet communication. With about a thousand meters of wire and fourteen trips up through the burned-out husk of Tube One, which requires an exposure suit and is basically a spacewalk since it passes a hole in the fuselage large enough to fly a shuttle through, she did it. We can't talk to those on the planet, and she thinks we never will, but we can hear them.

We all wish we couldn't.

I brought them to a planet full of dinosaurs.

My wife, my daughter, and my sons are trying to survive on a planet full of dinosaurs.

We huddle around the tinny speaker, listening to the voices below. In the main camp, First Officer Singh has taken charge. He's calling himself a general, and has appointed officers from the crew. Singh is a smart man. If they have a hope of survival, he'll find a way. And he's got Carthage to help him. Head of security on a spaceship of humans is a far cry from head of security on a planet full of man-eating reptiles, but Carthage is tough.

I believe my wife and children are still alive there. I haven't heard any of their voices, but I've heard them mention Josh and Caleb as part of the team that's setting up the electric wire perimeter. So I know that at least my boys are helping keep the rest of the colony alive.

There are a few other transports that survived the landing, but so far we haven't found a way to connect their signals to the main base, which they're calling Eden, and the irony of that is staggering to me. A few people are alive on a transport pretty near the base, and another landed on a beach some distance away. A third is just across the mountains, but there's a sea channel between them, so I suspect those folks are lost forever. That's a shame because Nirah Saffar is alive there, and if anyone could be useful in figuring out a way to survive in that jungle, it's Nirah.

Bethany will keep trying to find a way for us to communicate with them, but for the moment I'm glad we can't. They don't need to be worrying about us. Better that they think we're all dead so they can focus on their own survival down there.

Sunrise over the planet's edge is breathtaking out the little windows in the room I've taken as my own. Light bursts across the crescent of Ceti, and the galaxy behind it fades in the glory of the sun washing the land with gold. When it sets in a blur of colors, the dark sweep of sky returns and I can see a million other stars. The constellations here are different than our earth forefathers saw. Orion's belt is bent, but the great square of Pegasus is still visible. In the impossible distance, Earth's sun sits next to Arcturus. I can't pick it out from the window, but some nights I look back on that vast expanse of space. So many stars. So many worlds. So many other planets where we might have been aimed, if only our forefathers had known. They never would have sent us here if they had.

I think about our sister ships, the Beta and the Delta, both speeding off in opposite directions. What will they find in a few hundred years when they finally arrive at their destination planets?

Will they find a more hospitable world than Tau Ceti e? Will they find something worse than dinosaurs? Will they make it at all, or are the few terrified humans whose voices we cling to the very last of the human race?

CHAPTER 6

CALEB

There was no question that I was going. And no question that Shiro wasn't.

"I'll go. I can go. I can do it."

We walked down the dark hallway together toward our rooms. Mine was next to Mom's and Malia's. Shiro's was just down the hall from me. He had no other family since the cruel irony of finding his father only to lose him on the long walk back from the Seventeen landing site.

"I know you could," I answered him. "But we don't want to take many people. We don't know how many survivors there might be and we only have three zodiacs. The more of us there are, the more trips across the water we'll have to take to shuttle everyone across."

We didn't know if anyone was still alive from Transport Eight. But if there was a chance, and especially if Nirah might be among them, there was no discussion. We were Carthage. We were going.

I acknowledged the part of me that was thrilled about this.

Anyone else would have thought I was crazy. We were safe in our valley, protected by mountain peaks all around. It was possible to climb over, but the dinosaurs from the jungle outside wouldn't have survived the cold heights even if they'd wanted to. Everyone slept soundly in our warren of caves. And with the early warning system that was Ryenne's pet 'saurs, we hadn't lost anyone to a pterosaur attack since we'd returned to the valley. They would start laying eggs soon, we hoped. The more of the little fruit-eaters, the better.

But it was too quiet. Too comfortable. I wasn't meant to be a farmer, even though that's exactly what I *was* meant for. We all were. Primitives living off the land, with the rusting technology of a world two hundred years dead. We could live here. For me, it just wasn't the same as being alive. That only happened outside our safe mountain walls.

Shiro must have felt it, too, but he'd developed a deep phobia about the bodies of water on this planet. It had almost cost both of our lives. And as brave as he was, he was a terrible choice for this insane mission across the sea channel.

"If Nirah can fix the shuttle, maybe you can be part of the flight team."

He shrugged. "Maybe. Do they really think she's going to get that thing flying? And it doesn't just have to fly. It's got to launch." He leaned against the stone entrance to his room. "It's crazy. There's no way we'll ever get them back." He seemed to realize what he'd just said. "Sorry, Caleb."

I knew he was right. "It's okay. I know it. Just can't stop thinking about it, you know?" The ceiling of the cave was hung with luminescent stalactites, glowing soft blue. I looked up as if I could see through the tons of stone into the night sky. "He's been up there. All these years. They all have. Hoping we'd come and save them. And . . ." I trailed off.

"Don't give up. We haven't even started yet."

"Yeah. Long way to go before we give up."

★ ★ ★

It was decided that only five of us would go. Mayor Borin made it clear that I was the leader. For a moment I wondered if he was going to promote me, make me a sergeant or even a general. But it seemed we were done with military titles. Josh had volunteered along with Shiro, but the final group ended up as Kintan and Adam, along with Fernando, one of the men from Seventeen and . . . *Sigh*. Don Rand.

He was the logical choice. The only two engineers we had in Carthage were him and Mayor Borin. Obviously the mayor in his wheelchair wasn't an option. And Don had insisted. Knowing his daughter was alive on the Horizon had lit a fire under him. The man who tried to shove his way past women and children for a seat on the tank was now volunteering to hike forty kilometers through the mountains and cross a sea channel. Twice.

If Bethany wasn't up there, he wouldn't have gone. The prospect of rescuing more of our people would never have been enough to get him out of the safety of the valley. I just hoped they were still alive out there.

We had to travel light. The zodiacs folded into packs we could each carry, but we'd also need to take food, water, guns and ammunition, and the pack we were putting together with all the wire and spare sat trans we had. As heavily laden as we'd be, we figured it would take almost a week to get to the channel, assuming decent weather. And no dinosaurs.

There were some 'saurs in the mountains, small, fast moving beasts, but nothing dangerous. We had found a couple of steam vents in the distant reaches of our cavern systems, and Sara said the little 'saurs probably slept around other such vents to keep their body heat overnight. At least in the mountains we could travel by day. None of the big 'saurs would be anywhere near us.

I supervised the packing. Fernando was a big brute who could probably carry twice as much as I could. I was worried about his climbing skills, but if strength counted for anything, we'd be glad to have him.

"Handguns only," I said as we stood in the pathetic armory.

There was hardly anything left. No grenades. A couple of semi-automatic rifles with no ammunition. Nowhere near as many rounds for the pistols as I would have liked, but what choice did we have? "At least ten of the lightning sticks." Kintan bundled the electrified three-foot rods together. They were useful against the smaller 'saurs, but Sara was convinced they'd allow us to get across the sea channel. Then again, Sara wasn't going to be on the boats.

The trusty canteen that had seen me through so many nights in the jungle clipped on to my belt. I hitched my heavy pack onto my back.

We would be crossing our valley and heading up the north slope. Kintan checked his sat trans, marking the most likely path. We wouldn't have satellite coverage to tell us where we were, so staying on course was essential.

"Everybody ready?"

The sky was pink overhead, but the valley was still in shadow. It would be another hour before the sun rose over the peaks. I had said my goodbyes last night. *Josh will take care of Mom. And vice versa.*

Kintan's wife, one hand on her pregnant belly, walked with us to the top of the stone staircase. She clung to her husband until he gently peeled her arms off, and kissed her on the forehead. The citizens of Carthage were mostly still asleep as we trooped down off the plateau, past the fields and orchards, and began our journey north.

CHAPTER 7

CALEB

It only took us six days to reach the channel.

We started our journey clambering over one of the passes into our valley that we'd closed off with as much rock as we could manage to pile up. The sat trans wouldn't be terribly useful except to keep us moving in the right direction. We'd have to pick our way through the rocky hills, trying to find passable trails into the north.

Fernando carried two of the zodiacs. I carried the extra ammunition. We were all armed with pistols but nothing taller than waist-high skittered away from us. We kept to the lower passes but the nights were still chilly in the mountains. When the sun set and travel became dangerous, I wrapped myself in a wool blanket, pulling it up over my head to keep out the wind.

The plants that grew up here were low and scrubby, thorny bushes and twisting, gnarled trees pushing through the rocks. A small 'saur, one of the little rock-hoppers that climbed around our mountains, was stuck in a thick twist of thorn bushes. It was alive, breathing slowly, not struggling.

"Why's it just sitting there?" Fernando took a step toward the bush and I pulled him back.

"It's drugged. Sara says the thorns have some kind of poison in them. She's got some growing back at Carthage. Thinks she can maybe make some kind of painkiller out of it or something."

The little 'saur's head lolled back, eyes glazed.

Fernando crouched on the rocky ledge, eyeing the two-inch spikes that poked out of the brown vines crawling up the bare stone. "We could pull it out and eat it."

"No way," I said. "Don't reach in there. Not worth a scratch from those thorns. They go right through 'saur skin. They'll go right through yours."

"Rot it all, what is there on this planet that's not trying to kill us?"

I grinned. "Not a darned thing."

At regular intervals we marked the rocks with a thick, sappy paint. If by some miracle we managed to survive this trip, we'd want it to be easy to find our way home.

On the afternoon of the sixth day, we started heading downward. The salty smell of the sea drifted up into my nostrils, along with a fresh, green scent. We scrambled around a boulder on the hillside and saw the channel below us.

No way to do the tree trick here.

The sat trans image hadn't done it justice. It was wide—if it were land, it would take an hour to walk across it—slow moving, and dark. We'd been here long enough to know that slow, dark water meant deep. And deep meant dinosaurs.

"Sara was right. It's trees." Kintan nodded down at the land below us.

On each side of the channel, a flat plain of pine forest bordered the water. That was the green smell. The trans image had showed us the greenery, and Sara's plan relied on it. We'd need the wood to make the training rafts.

"Gonna be a ton of work to get across."

Don snorted. "Let's hope Sara was right about everything."

We descended onto the plain and drew our pistols as we crept into the trees. The trunks grew straight and tall, and thick needles made a soft carpet underfoot. Hardly any underbrush hindered our path. Nothing to hide a Crab. *And nothing to slow down a Wolf.*

But we didn't see a lot of 'saurs here. The little furry mammals we called shrews seemed to rule this area. I counted at least six different kinds of them, hopping between the branches above our heads and skittering away from our feet. At least we wouldn't starve.

"What are all these things?" Don peered into the trees, pistol raised. I hadn't wanted to give him a pistol, but couldn't come up with a compelling reason not to.

I shrugged. "We call them all 'shrews.' Good news is, when they're out in the open like this, it usually means there's no 'saurs around."

We approached the edge of the sea channel with caution. The water was muddy and dark. Don walked toward the edge and I caught his arm. "You don't want to get any closer than you need to."

It was unlikely that anything was waiting to lunge out of the water at us. This was a salt water channel, not fresh. 'Saurs and shrews wouldn't go to the edge to drink from a channel like this, so there wouldn't likely be anything lurking in the shallows. That was river behavior. And swamp. But Sara said there were likely as many different kinds of 'saurs living in the oceans as there were on land. We had no reason to think they'd be any friendlier. But we hoped they'd share some characteristics with their terrestrial cousins. Sara's idea depended on it.

"Let's sort out where we're going to sleep."

Sara speculated that dusk would be the best time for her plan to work. We couldn't cross in total darkness, and the full moon was weeks away. But we didn't want to do it in bright sunlight, either.

All our trust was in Sara's plan. She'd laid it out when we realized there was no way around this channel.

"We have to train the 'saurs in the water," she'd said, "and they only understand two things. Hunger and pain."

We'd looked at her blankly.

"Look," she'd said. "For the first couple of weeks after we landed here, the 'saurs kept walking right into our fence. They'd get zapped and it would spark, and they'd run off. Eventually most of them stopped running into it. They learned that it hurt to touch, and the meal they smelled inside wasn't worth it."

Shiro had raised an eyebrow. "Most of them did, yes. Not all of them."

"Right," Sara said. "But we only need a little window of safety. Just time to get across and back."

I had noted her use of "we." It wasn't going to be "we." It was going to be "me," and the thought had chilled me even then in the safety of the cave.

"We'll use a sound cue and a visual cue," she'd continued, grabbing one of our crudely-drawn maps and flipping it over to sketch on the back side. "We'll build something that floats . . . a little raft. A bunch of them. We'll wire up a sat trans and a lightning stick with a strobe light, something the 'saurs will have never seen before. And we'll make it sound like the engine on the boat will when it's time to actually cross." She nodded, drawing on the paper. "We'll drape wire so it hangs into the water along with the trans. When the 'saur bites it, he'll get a mouth full of electricity. It will take a couple of tries, but sooner or later he'll learn to avoid the noise and the strobe light."

Mayor Borin had looked at me. "That sounds far too risky. You're assuming there's only one 'saur in the water, which is ridiculous."

"It's not, though," Sara had replied. "Land 'saurs are territorial. Especially the big predators. There's no reason to think the ones in the water are any different. There should only be a couple in that stretch of channel. Once they learn to stay away from the strobe, the boats will be safe."

Returning to the present, I looked around the trees near the water's edge. "Kintan, maybe you and Adam can find a good couple of trees to make camp. Don't think we need to climb super-high, but we're not sleeping on the ground, even with a watch."

It would be dark here at night. Darker than the luminescent jungle full of glowing skitter slime. We wouldn't see anything hunting us at night.

Adam and Kintan dropped their packs and wandered off between the trees. In a few minutes they returned.

"Found a couple that should work," Kintan said, picking up his pack. We followed him to the site, three trees with low enough branches for us to jump into. Once we reached the branches, we'd have no trouble clambering through them into the higher boughs. Should be safe enough. *Unless something hunts in this kind of tree that we have no idea about.*

"I can't get up there." Don was looking at the trees Kintan had chosen.

Why did we bring him? "We can fix a couple of holds for you." Our packs contained some climbing equipment that we hadn't needed on our trek across the mountains. The little metal pitons would pound into tree bark just as well as into rocks. "Let's find some deadfall and start chopping."

We'd need a lot of wood, and not just to build a path for Don to get into his tree at night. Each of us pulled an axe out of our packs, and we headed deeper into the pine forest.

Once we rigged enough holds for Don to get up a tree, we set to building our dummies.

My axe bit into a downed branch, the first of many. "Adam, why don't you do first watch while the rest of us start work."

He hefted the rifle onto his hip and knelt on the ground with his back to the water, scanning the tree line up and down. Kintan, Fernando, and I started arranging the branches we'd gathered. Don flopped down onto the ground and dumped out the extra sat trans we'd brought, along with the long coil of thin wire and the lightning sticks.

I selected two branches. "Wish we had some kind of glue or something. This is going to take forever."

We laid out two long branches parallel on the ground, and started layering more across them, perpendicularly. Kintan pulled a bundle of twine out of his pack and started to lash the branches together. "Should we make a bunch of these before we start using them?"

I nodded. "Sara said we would probably need at least four or five. She said not to give up until we used all ten of the lightning sticks we brought. And I'm thinking we don't want to give them too much time between runs, so yeah, we need to build ten of them."

Adam looked over from where he knelt on the ground. "We only need to build seven. We have three zodiacs to rig. If we lose all ten sticks, we won't have any left to cross."

Twine burned my fingers as I pulled a knot tight, securing the little branch structure.

Kintan shrugged, stripping needles from another branch. "I hope we need all three on the way back. Hope we find two more zodiacs full of people."

I looked out over the slow-moving water. "We're using all three just for us on this crossing. Not putting all of us in one boat." I didn't need to say why. If Sara's plan didn't work, maybe we'd only lose one. Life on Ceti was all about risk management. Everything we did was an effort to ensure that somebody survived.

The sun was dipping behind the mountains as we finished the third raft. Don had the first one draped with wire, securing it to a lightning stick and wiring it onto one of the sat trans he'd rigged before we left Carthage. He tapped the power button and the trans lit up with a bright yellow flashing strobe from its screen. A loud, deep rumble played through its speaker.

Don nodded and shut it off, careful not to touch the exposed wire. "One down."

I called a halt to the work while the sky was still purple dusk. We trooped back to the trees we'd selected and hauled our supplies up, settling in for the night. We couldn't get as high as I wanted in these evergreens, but we hadn't seen anything except shrews since we came down out of the hills. Darkness fell quickly. The thin sliver of moon barely illuminated the rippling below.

This is the stupidest thing you've ever done. We don't even know for sure that anyone's still alive on the other side of that channel. I was alone in my tree, peering up through the thick needles. The tree was too dense to see into the sky where the star that wasn't a star glittered in the night. Horizon Alpha, the largest star in the sky. The dead ship that wasn't dead. For three long years I'd cursed the sight of it, imagining my father lying still and cold in one of its dead halls. Now I squinted toward the moon. *If you don't do this, you'll be right. Horizon will be his grave, just like you always thought.*

I looked out over the water now. So much darker than in the forest or the luminescent caves. Anything at all could be in that black water. Any number of anythings. If we worked all day tomorrow, by tomorrow evening we'd be ready to test Sara's theory. And if it looked like it was working, in a couple of nights we'd be out there in tiny boats, trusting a motor noise and a strobe light to keep us out of the jaws of a bloody, wet death.

CHAPTER 8

CALEB

By dusk the next day we were ready.

Most of the channel's edge was a three-meter drop from rock to water, but we'd chosen a spot where the ground sloped right down to the sea. It would be our testing ground, and if the plan worked, our boat launch.

Fernando hauled the first raft down onto the rocky shore. He eyed the water all around him, pushing the rickety structure out onto the surface.

First we see if the stupid things float.

A tiny, shameful part of me hoped the raft would sink. If we couldn't get them to float and train the water 'saurs to stay away from them, we wouldn't have to attempt this crossing. *And we won't have any chance at all of rescuing Dad. We'll just keep talking in Morse Code over the sat trans until they all die up there.* I took a deep breath.

The raft floated. We tied a length of twine from the raft to a large rock, tethering it with about thirty meters of slack.

Don reached out and turned on the sat trans, keeping his hands clear of the wires that attached it to the lightning stick and draped under the raft. He dropped the waterproof trans over the edge where it hung on a short length of wire into the water beneath the branches. The motor noise rumbled out of it.

"Okay. Push it on out. Don't touch the wires."

Fernando used another branch to shove the little raft out into the lazy current. We all stepped back from the edge and watched the blinking light drift out into the channel.

For a few moments there was nothing.

"Maybe nothing lives in this part of the water?" Don said.

With a great sucking splash, the raft disappeared. A huge gray mouth closed over the hole in the water, snapping the twine that attached the raft to the shore.

"Oh, my sweet . . ."

The water erupted and bits of pine branch shot up from the surface. A giant splash drenched our feet as the 'saur belched out the remains of the raft.

I chuckled. "Guess he didn't like it much."

Don's face was ghost-white, eyes huge. "How . . . how . . ."

"It's okay." I turned back to the higher ground where the rest of the rafts waited their turn to be devoured. "You don't have to go across. You can wait here. You just have to get us across." If we made it to the other side, at least we'd have a little while away from him.

The second raft made it further downstream before disappearing in a shower of sparks and pine.

Kintan shook his head. "This isn't working."

I shrugged. "It's the only plan we have. We're not going back to Carthage until we've used them all."

The third raft floated to the end of the length of twine. The sky was nearly dark and we could easily see the strobe light pulsing in the water below the little raft. It disappeared as something swam in front of it. The raft bumped, and the water around it churned. It stayed afloat.

We waited another ten minutes. Nothing touched the raft.

We hauled it back in on the twine and Don used a long piece of wood to pull the sat trans away from the electric wire before shutting it off so we could pull the raft from the water.

I looked up into the darkening sky.

We're coming, Dad. Hold on.

The next night we repeated the process. The first raft was destroyed, but the second stayed afloat for about five minutes before something flipped a huge, flat tail out of the water, making a giant wave that sank the raft. We watched it go down, strobe blinking into the darkness. We watched the water erupt when the strobe disappeared.

"Doesn't taste any better after you sink it," I muttered.

The third raft was untouched for almost an hour before we pulled it in.

Later we huddled together in the trees.

"All right. Tomorrow we do this." My words were met with silence.

"It's not going to get any better the longer we wait," I continued. "We want to do this while that zap is fresh in its mind."

Kintan grunted. "We're assuming that was all the same 'saur."

"Yep. But nothing went after that last raft. If there's more than one, they learned from watching the one that got zapped. Tomorrow we'll float two of them together, and if they're safe for an hour, we cross."

Don shifted in the tree. "I think . . . it would be better if I stayed here. I can . . . watch. You know."

"That's the plan," I agreed. "You stay here until we get across. Then head back to Carthage and let them know we made it." I didn't suggest what he'd tell them if we didn't make it. At least they'd know.

"Wait, you want me to go back alone?"

I sighed. "Yes. We might not cross back at exactly this same spot once we've found whoever is over there to find. I don't want to spend a week stomping up and down here trying to find you. And I have no idea how long we'll be over there. It doesn't make any sense for you to wait here. Just follow the paint marks on the rocks. We left a good trail from here."

We had three rafts left. If Sara's plan worked, we'd reel in the two decoys tomorrow night and pull the sat trans and lightning sticks from all three. We'd stash those for the return trip. The remaining unused three we would hang from the zodiacs, one for each, strobing away beneath us in the water, powering the electric wires that were all that stood between us and a very quick death.

I was used to sleeping in trees. But the pine needles dug into my back and the quiet of this strange forest poked into my nerves. Sleep did not come that dark night.

CHAPTER 9

CALEB

We wired up the zodiacs at dusk. The land across the water looked far too open for my liking; not a pine forest like this side, but a scattering of trees on a scrubby, flat ground. The beacon we were following, sent to us by Horizon, showed our target just over a dozen kilometers of rocky hills away. If not for the water, we would be there already.

Kintan kept a watch on the forest at our backs as we launched the two lashed-together rafts. While they floated untouched in the slow current, we finished the final preparation on the zodiacs, wiring in the sat trans and electricity to each one. Fernando would ride with me, and Kintan and Adam would drive their own boats alone since Don wasn't making the crossing with us. We would stay close, but not so close that if one of our craft was lost, the others couldn't make a run for safety.

This is insane. This is stupid. This is ridiculous.

We hauled in the rafts and pulled the sat trans and lightning sticks from each one, tucking one each into separate packs along with the wire. Just in case. Each zodiac had a small motor which we tested now, holding the little propellers up out of the water. They had worked when we tested them back at Carthage, and they worked now. There was enough room to load the rafts onto the zodiacs, which would save us time on the return trip, not having to build new ones. Assuming the water 'saurs remembered the lesson and didn't crunch up the rafts when we were ready to cross back. Assuming we made this first crossing at all.

Don stood on the shore well back from the watercraft. "Okay. You guys be careful. I'm heading up into the hills while there's still a little bit of light left." He practically ran off through the pines, heading for the path we had marked on the way in. We were far enough north that we'd lost satellite coverage here. Finding Transport Eight would rely on us following the map we'd set out back at Carthage. If we didn't return to this exact crossing, it might add days to our trip if we ended up off course on the way back.

"Are we ready?" Adam squinted out over the rapidly darkening water.

This is stupid.

"Yeah. I think we're ready."

We set the zodiacs into the water and turned on the sat trans strobe lights, lowering them on rope into the water beneath each boat. I splashed in up to my knees, clambering over the side of the Zodiac and pushing off into deeper water. Fernando hesitated, looking back to where Don had disappeared.

"Let's go. It's getting dark already."

Fernando grunted and leaped from the shore, bouncing into the boat. Kintan and Adam flanked me, one on each side. We started our engines and began the slow crawl across the channel.

The movement of the water under the boat turned my stomach. I was the only person on Ceti who had ever gone into the water and survived. My throat closed up at the memory of washing down a fast river, clawing at the water and scrambling for air. It was a feeling I never wanted to repeat.

The strobe lights below flashed deep into the water, lending an eerie, erratic glow to our progress.

A bright reflection under Kintan's boat caught my eye and I squinted into the depth. The next strobe flashes showed only dark water.

"What? What are you looking at?" Kintan's voice was high and tight over the grumble of the zodiac motors.

I shook my head. "Nothing. Just keep going."

The shore was forever away. I glanced behind me. A quarter of the way. Fernando gripped the straps on the zodiac's edge, kneeling at the front of the boat, peering over the edge into the water below.

Night was falling quickly. My eyes couldn't adjust to the dark distance of the far shore over the bright flashes of the strobes beneath us. My head whipped around, peering from Adam's boat to Kintan's, then back to the distant, dim shoreline.

The reflection flashed under Kintan's boat again. *Don't say anything. Don't scare him. Nothing he can do.* I pulled my zodiac a little closer to his, and Adam responded by tightening the distance to my boat. Maybe we'd look more intimidating if we were close together. One big scary flashing electric surface monster instead of three smaller ones.

"What was that?" Kintan's boat rocked as something touched it from below.

"Hang on!" I yelled, helpless to do anything but pilot my own boat and watch.

A huge wave shot up behind him as whatever had bumped him splashed a giant tail. Kintan's boat shot forward in the surge and mine jolted to the right. I grabbed at my pack, catching it before it slopped over the side, gripping on to the motor's handle. A muffled curse told me Adam had also been hit by the wave. Saltwater burned my eyes.

Kintan's boat was well ahead of mine and Adam's now, too far to yell across. It was too dark for me to see him clearly, but he was still in the zodiac, clinging onto the motor just like I was. We plowed forward. Fernando had dropped into the bottom of our boat and was muttering to himself.

Over halfway there.

My heart pounded, eyes watering from the salt dripping off my hair.

It flipped the tail because it got the shock. If this was the same 'saur that had bitten into the first few sets of electric wires, that should be enough. Sara had counted on it, and now our lives depended on it.

We had left too late. I could barely see the shoreline now. The dim moonlight wasn't enough to judge our distance. What were we heading for? Rocks? A seawall we wouldn't be able to climb? I looked from left to right, forward and behind. *Come on. Come on. Where is the scatting land?*

I heard a crunch up ahead. Kintan's strobe light bobbled under his zodiac.

I waited for the splash, for the zodiac to disappear in a great, sucking swallow of churning water and teeth.

It didn't come. The light disappeared for a moment, then reappeared. It waved from side to side in the air.

"He's made it! He's on shore!"

Adam and I raced for the beacon. When my zodiac crunched into the rocky shore, I tumbled headfirst into Fernando.

"Careful! We need these to get back." Kintan waved the sat trans and Adam crashed into the shore right next to me. We scrambled out of the watercraft and dragged them onto dry ground, careful not to touch the wires that hung from the bottom.

It worked. Sara's plan worked. We had made the crossing alive.

We spent the night near the shoreline. It was far too dark to travel after sunset, and I found myself missing the soft blue glow of the deep jungle. Our bioluminescent caves were never this dark. I could barely tell if my eyes were open or closed. We didn't dare make a fire or use the lights on our sats. Any big 'saur could hunt this scrubby plain at night. We hadn't seen anything big enough to worry about since leaving Carthage, but this was a different kind of terrain than we'd just crossed from. It was like a whole new planet. A dark one.

There wasn't much point in keeping watch since we couldn't actually see, but we took turns staying awake that night, listening to every noise on the shore. Insects chirped and buzzed all around. The sound was comforting and familiar. In the deep jungle when an apex predator was near, everything fell silent. Was that true on this side of the channel? I didn't know.

I slept fitfully on the hard ground and was awake well before the first glow of dawn. My pack was still loaded with dried fruit and meat strips and I chewed quietly as the land around me brightened.

Kintan was still asleep and I nudged him with my foot. He jumped at the touch, eyes popping wide.

"Just me. Time to move."

We gathered our packs and deflated the zodiacs, folding them down into their travel cases. Fernando picked up all three.

"Everybody ready?"

Nods all around. Fernando kept looking back at the water, but I was peering into the brush. Still too early for most of the 'saurs. Maybe no 'saurs even here. But there was a lot more plant life on this side. Plants meant herbivores. And herbivores meant carnivores.

There was no gentle slope into the hills here, but a sudden change from scrubby growth to jutting rock. We followed the rock north, paralleling the sea channel, looking for a pass into the mountains. The map we had loaded onto the trans was not detailed enough for us to find a way. And if we got too far off course, we would never have a hope of finding Transport Eight. If anyone was even still alive there. Which would make last night's water crossing a complete waste of time and effort. *At least we all made it over alive. One step at a time.*

"I think we can get up here." Adam led us up a narrow trail into the rocky hills. I didn't like trails. 'Saurs used trails. Fernando followed Adam, with Kintan and me in the rear. We all had pistols tucked into the backs of our pants, for all the good they'd likely do.

I felt better the higher we got. Kintan kept his eyes on the map and we marked our trail with paint just as we'd done on the other side of the water.

A few hours in, a bright reflection caught my eye. Something shiny, wedged between a couple of rocks. Kintan had walked right past it, and must have brushed against it with his pants leg. It wiped off the thick, brown grit in a little smear, revealing the gleam of metal.

"Hey, guys, check this out." I knelt next to the rocks and brushed at the thing. It was round and smooth, roughly egg-shaped, and about as long as my arm. Scratchy, regular marks were revealed as I wiped off the dirt.

I'd seen something like this before, stuck in the swamp the day the General had been killed. We hadn't had any idea what the scratchy marks meant then. I still couldn't read them, but Sara could. *Birdman writing.* She'd be over the moon. I snapped a photo with my sat trans.

"What is that thing?" Adam eyed it, backing away. "Don't touch it."

"It's something from the Birdmen." I spat on the silver egg and wiped at the writing. "Anybody read Birdman?"

Everyone shook their heads.

"Help me move it." I strained to pick it up but there was no way I could lift it. The thing was smooth all the way around except for the writing. No ridge that might allow it to open, just the scratchy symbols. Fernando helped me shift it, revealing more writing on the other side, caked with dirt.

Kintan squatted next to me. "It's cool, but we need to keep moving. It's too heavy to take with us. Just get some pictures for Sara and let's go."

I kept wiping the thing down, revealing the markings from the bottom. They were regular hash marks, all in a line. First one, then two, then three, and so on down to nine. The next line was a diagonal slash, followed by a tiny X. At the very bottom was a perfect circle with a diagonal line dividing it in half. All the figures were etched into the surface of the silver egg.

My fingernails dug out the grime in the symbols. When I touched each one, it glowed briefly.

"Hey, look at this!" I demonstrated, touching each line. A pale red glow lit each set of hash marks as my finger squeaked down the egg's surface.

Adam grabbed my shoulder. "Caleb, don't touch that. Who knows what it is? What if it's a bomb or something?"

I hadn't thought of that. But . . . no. The Birdmen wouldn't leave a bomb just sitting here. Or in the swamp. "No way it's a bomb. No clue what it is, but it's been here a long time. Would have exploded by now."

Kintan touched one of the lines. "It's like . . . well, it's obviously numbers. One through nine, and maybe that diagonal line is supposed to be zero. So . . . maybe it's like a combination lock? A secret code or something?"

A Birdman code. But how were we supposed to crack it? And what would we find if we did? I searched the sides again, looking for some indication that it might open if the right code was entered. Nothing. Maybe Adam was right. Maybe this thing was a bomb, and the code would set it off.

I took pictures from every angle and stood up. "Well, it's way too heavy to bring back. Guess it will stay another Birdman mystery."

We shuffled away up the steep, rocky hill.

The twelve-kilometer journey took us three days. With every climb, every shimmy between boulders, I hoped against hope that the survivors we found at Eight would be able to make it back. *Please, no babies. No old people. Nobody injured.*

We paused past midday on the third day, crowding into the shade of an overhanging rock. My eyes were gritty and my mouth tasted like dirt.

"We have to be close." Kintan peered at the map. "We got a little too far north, but I thought we corrected." He peered down the cut between the rocks that we were following. "If I'm right, we should be no more than half a kilometer away. That way."

I looked in the direction he was pointing, straight through a boulder. "Do you see a way to get there?"

He shrugged. "We'll find it as we go."

Our water was getting low. We hadn't found a good clear stream to refill since we got to this side of the channel. I sipped instead of gulping like my body begged me to do.

We climbed and shuffled for three more hours until we were heading due west into the setting sun.

"I think we're going in circles," I grumbled. My foot slipped on a rock and I stumbled, scraping my elbow on a sharp stone.

"We're close now," Kintan muttered.

"You've been saying that for hours." Adam sounded as crabby as I felt.

"Well what do you want to do, turn back?"

I pulled up sharply at the angry tone. "Of course not." A deep sigh blew past my dry lips. "It's my dad up there. Of course I don't want to turn back."

"Then shut up and climb. We're close. I know it." Kintan scrambled up over a boulder.

He stared into a deep crevasse. The unmistakable glint of metal reflected up from the rocks below.

"No. It can't be . . ."

Adam and Fernando moved in behind us. They stood silently, staring at the wreckage of one of our transports. It was spread all over the hill, in large pieces and small.

Oh, no. This can't be them.

But it was someone. People I had grown up with, known all my life aboard Horizon had been on this transport, whichever one it was. Maybe kids like I had been when we landed here, what felt like a million years ago. Maybe friends of my parents. Maybe Kintan or Fernando's families.

I looked down into a ravine where a large chunk of hull had

settled. Scorch marks blackened the metal around huge holes where it had shattered off its wings. "Can you see a number anywhere?"

Kintan shook his head. "But Horizon said they heard them talking on their sat trans just a few months ago."

It couldn't be Nirah's group. No one could have survived this crash.

Fernando looked over the wreckage. "Maybe there were two transports?"

That had to be it. There were still at least five transports unaccounted for since the hasty launch from a burning mothership. We knew some of them probably hadn't made it safely to the ground. Surely this wasn't the one that was carrying my father's only hope of salvation.

"Should we . . ." Adam couldn't take his eyes from the twisted hunks of metal. "Should we look for survivors?"

I shook my head. "Not here. There's no one here." Whoever they were, they had been our people. More casualties of the hospitality of Tau Ceti e. Names on a wall in a cave.

We trooped on past the crevasse, shoulders slumped, feet shuffling. The sun was almost below the high peaks, throwing deep shadows over our twisting path.

If we don't find them soon, we'll have to stop for another night. And then what? My throat closed at the thought of giving up. But what if that really was their transport? What if Horizon was wrong and Nirah had been dead all this time? All the people back home hoping their loved ones might be coming back across the channel with us would be crushed when we returned alone. *And Dad will die on a dead ship in a black sky.*

"Hey guys?" Kintan's voice echoed in the rocky pass. "Get up here."

I followed him up and around a corner and found him standing on top of a rock, looking into a little valley. It was nowhere near as big as Carthage. It wasn't green and fertile, but brown and scrubby like the hills we'd been climbing through for three days. And sitting right in the middle was the hulking, dull metal shape of Horizon Alpha Transport Eight.

CHAPTER 10

CALEB

We ran straight into Mr. Chen. He was almost at the bottom of the path around a blind corner in a shadow, digging under a rock with a small metal pick. I had taken the lead of our little party and stumbled right over the top of him. He screamed and jumped back, raising the pick in defense.

"It's me," I said, hands up. "Caleb Wilde."

He dropped the pick and stared at me. His mouth opened in silent shock and he sank to his knees, tears bursting from his eyes.

"Oh, stars, are you real?"

I knelt next to him and picked up his tool. "We're real. We're here. How many are you?"

His hands were gnarled as he grabbed my arm, squeezing as if to test whether I was flesh or some kind of mirage. "We're . . . There are twelve of us now. Where have you been? We've waited so long. We thought there was nobody else left." He wiped his nose on the sleeve of his shirt, eyes darting among us.

I helped him stand and handed back his pick. "Let's go find

the rest, okay?"

It must have been such a shock to him. After three years alone up here enduring who-knew-what, we'd just appeared out of literally nowhere. My party had known we were looking for survivors up here. His party thought they were the only ones on the planet.

We followed him down into the valley. Someone must have seen us coming, and by the time we reached the plain, eleven other people were waiting. They rushed up to greet us, laughing and crying. A deep, joyous noise escaped Fernando's throat as he embraced a young woman, picking her up in a tight hug and swinging her around.

"Carmen! You're here!"

Fernando's sister squealed, wrapping her arms around her brother's neck. My eyes felt hot and I knuckled away my own tears, remembering the days on Horizon Alpha, which seemed like a million years ago. Shiro would sure be glad to see Carmen.

I scanned the little crowd until I saw the object of our search. Nirah Saffar. She looked older and more tired than I remembered from Horizon. I was just a little kid then, but she was one of my father's officers, in charge of everything mechanical on Horizon Alpha. Her dark hair was shot through with gray, but her eyes were steel.

"Where have you come from?" She took both my hands in hers. "Who is still alive?"

"There are almost a hundred of us now," I said, smiling. "We live in a huge green valley, and we've come to take you there."

"Did you lose your leader?"

I misunderstood her question. "We've lost a lot of people. Sam Borin is our current leader."

She looked behind me up the hillside. "Is he coming?"

Oh. She meant, who's leading this little party.

"No, he's back at our valley. I'm the leader of this rescue mission."

A gust of wind blew Nirah's hair into her face. "You are? I remember you from the ship. You're, what . . . sixteen?"

Heat flushed my face. "I've spent more time in the wilds of

this planet than anyone. I'm part of the Carthage advisory council. And yes, I'm sixteen."

She shook her head and frowned at the dimming sky. "Let's get back to the ship. You must be hungry."

We followed them back to their transport which lay on the hard ground, its nose partially buried in the dirt. None of our landings had been easy. Transport Eight's appeared to have almost been disastrous.

Nirah led us into the dim interior and someone pulled the door shut behind us. The transport's solar power still worked, and the interior was lit. They had pulled out all the seats and turned it into a bunkhouse of sorts. Old seat cushions were laid on the floor of the passenger area. It smelled of old, sour sweat and drying meat. The hatches to the cargo area behind and the cockpit ahead were closed and we all crowded together on the cushions.

"Why do you close the outside door?" I asked. "Is there anything that hunts here at night?"

Nirah shook her head. "No. There are a bunch of reptiles that hop around the hills. A wide variety of small mammals, all of which we can eat. But nothing we're afraid of until the flood." She cocked her head to the side. "Why? Is there something that hunts at night where you live?"

She doesn't even know. How can they not know? But there weren't any big 'saurs in the hills. We hadn't seen any fliers since we'd gotten into the higher mountains, either. If they'd never ventured south into the jungle, how would they know?

Adam beat me to the punch. "Oh, nothing much. Just dinosaurs. Lots and lots of dinosaurs."

That got the reaction he must have been hoping for. The next hours were spent telling our respective stories.

They had been here since they landed, never venturing far from the transport. They had been as far as the channel we'd crossed to the southeast, and a short way west, which was just more brown, dry hills. With no satellite signal, they had no idea where to begin searching for other survivors, and assumed there weren't any. They had seen the wreckage of Transport Three in the crevasse and thought we had all likely met the same fate. It was a hard existence here. Food was hard to come by, and the streams only flowed during the rainy season. But they were safe. Despite the odds, they were alive.

Something Nirah had said bounced around my brain.

"You said you're not afraid of anything until the flood? Does this valley flood when it rains?" I couldn't imagine enough rain to fill this whole area, but there wasn't much soil to absorb it.

"Not a water flood," she said. "It's a—a migration, we think. First full moon every year after spring equinox. Should be . . ." She thought for a moment. "In about sixty days. Right after Tau Ceti d rises this year. Don't you get them where you live?"

I shook my head. We were sitting propped up against the wall of the transport eating some kind of dried, crunchy bits out of a bowl made from an old helmet. I didn't really want to know what I was eating. *Probably bugs.* "I don't know what you're talking about."

"But you live in the mountains, right? I can't imagine they don't come where you are."

Kintan said, "We've only been there a couple of months."

She nodded. "Well, you need to be ready. Borin will have to figure something out, and fast. Near as we can figure, they nest around the hot springs up north. At some point the little ones hatch. They come over the mountains all together—hundreds of thousands of them. They eat everything they find. The first year . . . we had no idea they were coming. Almost seventy of us had landed here, and by the time the Flood came we'd only lost eight people. They killed over forty of our people before the rest of us could get inside and lock down the transport. It's just a swarm. Tiny reptiles, so quick. Like a plague. They swarm everywhere for days, moving on past like a flood." She closed her eyes and shook her head. "The second year we only lost five people before we realized what was happening. We hadn't stockpiled enough food, and it was an awful week, locked in here while they streamed around the portholes. Last year we were ready and didn't lose anyone."

Adam's eyes were wide. "Where do they go? We never saw them in the jungle."

Nirah shrugged. "They disappear south. We've been far enough to see there's a river down there, so that's probably where they go to breed. Very likely they have a specific migratory pattern, like birds back on Earth did. If they didn't come through where you were, thank your lucky stars. When they come back through a few weeks later, they don't eat anything. Their numbers are less than half, and they're fat and slow, full of eggs. Pretty tasty, actually. We think they go back up north, lay their eggs, and then probably die. There were apparently Earth insects that did that kind of thing."

"But these aren't insects? They're 'saurs?" I nodded, thinking how sad Sara would be not to get to study them.

"I wouldn't call them dinosaurs, no," she said. "But I guess they must be. No bigger than your palm. But thousands. Absolutely devastating in numbers." She waved toward the front of the cargo hold, where strips of dried meat were piled high. "We've got a good enough stockpile for this year."

I looked around the transport. "So you just hide in here while they pass?"

She nodded again. "You can hear them all over the transport. A few of them get in, but a few of them isn't a problem. Do you have enough transports in your valley for everyone to be safe when they come?"

"We don't have any transports. We live in the caves."

Her face paled. "Oh, no. You can't go in the caves."

Kintan scooted in next to Nirah. "We know. But our caves don't have the bloodsuckers. The Birdmen exterminated them."

Nirah paused. "The . . . Birdmen?" She glanced around at the rest of her people, all hanging on our words. Her expression clearly indicated that she thought we'd been climbing in the hot sun too long.

We told her what we knew about the alien species that once tried to colonize this planet. Everyone was huddled together, the mystery food forgotten.

Nirah smiled. "Seems there's a whole lot more to Ceti than we ever dreamed."

CHAPTER 11

CALEB

We talked into the night, sharing our stories. The people of Transport Eight were divided about coming back to Carthage with us. Some of them felt they were doing all right where they were.

"We've got food, water, and shelter," one of the older men said. "We don't have dinosaurs or whatever these bird people are. Why should we leave here just because these kids want us to come?"

Nirah frowned at him. "You're right, Ed. We do have what we need to survive. But look around. We thought we were the only humans on this planet. That we'd live what was left of our time, and die here alone." She looked around at her people, all thin and hollow-eyed. "There's no future here for us. When we're gone from here, we're gone. At their colony, though . . ." She looked at us with hope, and a little doubt. "Maybe we could do more than live out our days. Maybe we could be part of the future."

Nirah glanced over at Carmen Orellana, Fernando's younger

sister. She was leaning against her brother, and dropped her eyes at Nirah's look.

Nirah gave a small, sad smile. "Maybe Carmen wants a future."

She didn't have to elaborate. There weren't enough people from Transport Eight to create a viable colony on their own. They needed us just like we needed them.

In the end, the vote was almost unanimous. Two of the older men voted to stay in this valley, and everyone else voted to join us.

They were electric in their hope. We had brought them a dream they had never thought possible since crashing on this planet alone.

Looking around at their faces, I was struck by the weight of their newfound optimism. Let's just get back safely. All of us. I pushed my doubts aside and welcomed the future citizens of Carthage.

In the morning we packed up most of the meat they'd stockpiled, and the few tools they'd made from the remains of their transport. Theirs was one of the first transports loaded and launched in the chaos of Horizon's evacuation, and it was only meant to transport humans. Other transports had been packed with supplies, but the people of Transport Eight had little more than the clothes they were wearing, whatever personal items they'd managed to grab on the way out, and the basic life-support standard on the ships.

Nirah was shocked to learn that anyone was still alive on Horizon. "Guess that's our good luck then, isn't it?" We stood at the edge of their valley looking back at their wrecked ship. "If you hadn't made contact with them, you'd never have known we were here. Never come to look for us way up north."

And honestly, if we didn't need you to fix our last shuttle to go get them, we would never have risked the channel crossing to come find you. I didn't say that aloud, of course. But there was no way we would have braved that water if Nirah hadn't been our best hope of rescuing the remaining survivors.

Thank the stars there were no babies or old people among the

Transport Eight crew. I had been dreading what we might find, fretting over how we'd get the very young or infirm over the high, rocky hills back to the channel, and then over the mountains into Carthage. At least everyone here was strong enough to make the journey. There weren't enough canteens for everyone to have one, so now I worried that we'd run out of water before we got back to our side of the channel.

"Everybody try not to drink if you don't have to," I cautioned before we set out. "Hopefully we'll find some running streams along the way, but it's three days back to the channel, and we can't cross until dusk."

We hadn't made a big deal about the dangers that lurked in the channel. No sense worrying them unnecessarily. I felt a bit guilty about that, but there was no reason to share my fears about the journey and the crossing. It was a weight I could carry alone.

The marks we had painted on the rocks helped us on the way back. Kintan's pathfinding had been pretty spot-on, and looking at the mountain peaks we skirted, I realized he'd brought us the most direct way possible.

Carmen walked in front of me, just behind Fernando. She spoke over her shoulder as we climbed. "So . . . how many people did you say are at your valley?"

"Almost a hundred," I answered. "We just got your brother's group a little while ago from where they landed. And the rest of us all landed together."

"So . . . who all is there?"

I knew exactly who she meant by "who all." But I decided to drag it out a while. "Well, my brother Josh made it, and my mom and my little sister. My mom just had a baby, so that's cool, too. And Mr. Borin, Brent's dad . . . we just elected him Mayor."

Carmen's foot slipped on a rock and she cursed, scrambling at the sharp stones. "I remember Brent. How's he doing?"

Fernando reached down and pulled his sister up to the ledge he was standing on. "Brent's not there." He must not have heard the whole story of that final mission into the jungle.

"No," I said. "Brent didn't make it. He died trying to save us all." It was the same thing I'd told Brent's dad.

"Save you from what?"

"Um . . ." I hopped up behind them. "You remember I said there were dinosaurs here, right?"

She shrugged. "Yeah, we've seen a bunch."

I grinned. "Little ones, yes. Once you get out of the hills, there are . . . bigger ones."

We followed the rest of the group on up the climb.

"So . . . is Shiro around?"

Oh, thank the stars. She hasn't forgotten him. I was certain he hadn't forgotten her. I thought about stringing her along for a while, but that would just be cruel. "Sure is. He wanted to come on this mission, but we didn't want to bring any more people than necessary."

She paused on the rock and I was shocked to realize she was crying. Fernando met my eyes and we shared a "What's going on?" expression. In a few moments she composed herself. "It's just . . . I lost everybody. Everybody. And now you're here . . ." She smiled up at her brother. "And Shiro's alive. It's just a lot to take in."

Fernando hugged her and I felt a bit of moisture in my own eyes. *Don't let it fall. We can't afford the water.* "I get it. Felt the same way when I realized my dad hasn't been dead for the past three years."

We climbed for the next two days, not making much actual distance, but covering a lot of vertical ground. The strips of dried meat got harder and harder to chew as the hours passed. On the third morning we found a small drip of water, a rivulet dripping through a crack in the rocks. We took turns sucking at the moisture on the rock, but there wasn't enough flow to fill our canteens.

The next morning we were well into the descent. Our progress had been faster than I anticipated since we were able to follow the marked path. It was still early in the day when we paused on a wide ledge. Kintan was kneeling next to a couple of big rocks, and I recognized the glint of the Birdmens' silver egg-thing.

"Well, it hasn't exploded, so I guess it's not a bomb." I crouched next to him and Nirah, who was running her fingers over the markings.

"They're obviously numbers," she murmured, looking like a child with a birthday gift. "It has to be a code of some kind." She turned to me. "There's writing on the back?"

I nodded. "Yeah, but I can't read it. Only Sara can."

"Sara Arnson?" Nirah smiled. "No wonder you're all still alive. That's one smart lady."

"She says the same about you." I called up the photo of the writing from the backside on my sat trans. "See? It's definitely their writing. It's all over our caves. And we figured out it was numbers. We think the diagonal slash is a zero."

Nirah stared at the shining silver egg. "Is that the way they usually write numbers? With nine little lines to mean 'nine?'" She shook her head. "No way they would do math like that. They're space travelers. Physics we never dreamed of. Why would they write it like this? And what's this symbol?" She touched the perfect circle with the straight line bisecting it. Unlike the numbers and the little X, it didn't light up when she touched it. "A circle," she muttered. "Why is this here?"

I pulled a strip of meat from my pack and chewed, thinking. "We think it's like a combination lock. Maybe there's something inside if we can figure out the code."

She frowned. "Maybe. But why would they write it in such an elementary fashion? It's like they wanted it to be . . ." She trailed off, finger tracing the circle. In a moment she looked up, meeting my eyes. "Do you think they mean harm to other species?"

What a strange question. I thought about it, then answered, "No, I don't think so. They obviously had superior tech. They could have wiped all the 'saurs off this planet, but they didn't. Just found a safe place to live. They only left because their eggs didn't hatch here."

Kintan said, "Maybe it's the speed of light? Try that."

She shook her head. "The speed of light is always the same, of course, but the number would depend on what you measured it in. Meters per second? Why would we ever assume they would measure things in meters exactly the same as ours? No, it has to be something universal if it's meant to be a code left for someone else." She touched the circle with the line through it again. "Of course." She grinned. "I think I know what this means. I'm going to try it."

Before Adam could protest, her fingers touched the first number, a three. She said, "I think this little X is a decimal point." She touched it and it lit up.

Three. Little X. One. Four.

I knew that number, and suddenly the circle symbol made sense. "It's Pi! It's showing the diameter of a circle!"

Nirah's fingers continued touching the numbers, beyond the decimal places I knew by heart. One. Five. Nine. Two. "Exactly. It's the one universal mathematical number. Any species that uses base-10 math would calculate it the same way." Six. Five.

The egg's numbers all lit up at once.

We all backed away as the numbers began to pulse, fading on and off by themselves.

"Well," I said, staring at the glowing symbols, "you sure did something."

Adam edged over the side of the rock ledge, and several people followed him. I stayed next to Nirah, watching the egg light up, on and off.

After a few long minutes Fernando sighed. "It's not opening."

My shoulders sagged. "No, it's sure not opening."

Nirah crouched down next to it again, touching the numbers, but nothing changed. Just a slow on and off. "Are you sure we can't bring this with us?"

"No way." I nodded at Fernando. "Even he can't lift the thing. Whatever it is, it stays here."

We recorded a few minutes of it blinking on and off before reluctantly continuing our descent. Nirah and I were the last to leave the ledge and I almost had to push her away to get her over the side. "There's tons more Birdman stuff back at our caves. Sara just found a bunch of new rooms with more writing and drawings. Once we get the Horizon crew back, you can spend the rest of your life putting it all together."

The silent egg continued its blinking as we climbed away down the mountain.

CHAPTER 12

CALEB

We reached the bottom of the hills in the early afternoon. The smell of salt water had given way to the view of the wide channel, with green pine forest on the other side.

I didn't like this side one bit. Thick and brushy, the bit of flat ground offered plenty of cover for predators and nowhere for us to climb to safety. The rocks here weren't steep enough to deter a predator, either; we would have to climb quite a ways to escape anything chasing us. Everyone was hot and thirsty. We would be an easy meal if something found us.

We gathered at the edge of the rocks.

"All right," I said. "We need to make the crossing tonight. Everybody with a tool, let's cut some of the thicker branches off these bushes so we can make a couple of rafts." The Eight survivors had heard the story of Sara's success in getting us across the channel.

Nirah nodded. "And everyone who doesn't have a tool, gather up the canteens and head down the channel. There has to be a stream draining into it somewhere."

"No way." I grabbed the arm of the man nearest me, one of the older men from Eight, Ed Braxton. "Nobody leaves the group. The more we spread out, the greater the chance that something will smell us or hear us. We're dead meat if any of the bigger 'saurs find us here." I squinted up at the sun. Being out on the flat like this in daylight was risky, but we had to get the rafts together. We'd been gone from the channel for a week. The water 'saurs might have forgotten our lessons.

Nirah looked down her nose at me. "You boys may be used to running around with no supplies, but my people need water."

You boys? I gritted my teeth. *Here we go.*

"Nirah, I understand. We're all thirsty." Her eyebrows raised when I called her by her first name. "But you need to understand that I know this kind of terrain a lot better than you do. I know the dangers here, and running out of water is the least of our worries. We didn't run into anything on our way up these hills, but there are 'saurs out here that could kill every single one of us. We need to get over this channel and up into the hills on our side. There's water there. It won't be a pleasant day, but it's what we have to do."

Something splashed in the channel and we all turned to look, but there was nothing but a big ripple.

Kintan was already pulling wire out of his pack. "Caleb's right. I don't like this place." He glanced around at the high grasses and scant cover. "Nowhere to hide out here."

"I know you think you know best." Nirah sounded like she was talking to a child. "But you are not the leader of my people. I'm the ranking Horizon Alpha officer and it's my responsibility to get my people to safety. To do that, we need water." She addressed three of the women. "Gather the canteens and head downstream. Find us some water while the rest of us"—she looked at me condescendingly—"build rafts."

The three women took the few canteens that the rest of the Eight survivors carried. None of the Carthage crew offered ours. There was nothing I could do, and I watched them scuffle off down the edge of the rocks.

I turned to my crew. "Get the zodiacs wired right now."

The rest of the Transport Eight survivors didn't seem to know what to do. I showed them the right kind of branches to cut from the scrubby little trees and took everyone near the water's edge to begin lashing the branches together. The sun was still high and I figured we had about three hours until dusk when we would launch our rafts. If they went unmolested in the water, we would cross tonight. If they were swallowed up, we might have to wait another night. Maybe Nirah was right. *We will need more water if we have to go another day.* We'd climb back into the hills to wait out tomorrow if we had to. Nowhere near enough cover to be safe here.

Fernando, Kintan, and Adam each wired up a zodiac while I instructed everyone else on making the rafts.

My hands froze on the lashing as a human scream echoed through the flat valley.

Nirah was not right.

We pulled our weapons, squinting out over the bushes. Two of the three women who had gone out with canteens were sprinting back toward us. As we watched in horror, the one in the rear was pulled down by a flash of gray. I couldn't see for sure what got her in the tall grass, but the glimpse was enough to make the hairs on the back of my neck stand up.

Oh, scat.

"Get the zodiacs in the water right now!"

My crew obeyed my shout.

The remaining woman stumbled into the group, gasping for air. "They're . . . we didn't . . . Kim was . . ." She collapsed onto the ground, hyperventilating. Nirah knelt next to her.

I wasn't positive what had taken the two women down, but whatever it was, she had led it right to us. *Maybe there's only two of them, and they've each got a meal now.*

My optimism was shattered by a noise in the brush.

Click.

"Into the water, get on and launch right now." I whispered

the words, but everyone heard. My crew had heard the click and were already pulling at the people nearest them, trying to guide them onto the zodiacs. The Eight people had no idea what that noise meant.

"There's not enough room," one of them said. "We need to make two trips. And you said it should be dark . . ."

I shoved him onto a boat and grabbed the next person in line.

"Now. Now, now, now, now." They must have understood the terror in my voice, because they scrambled onto the zodiacs, huddling together to make room.

Click.

Kintan's boat with Nirah on it was already a little way out in the channel. My zodiac was loaded and I stood in knee-deep water, waiting for Adam to get the last of his people on. Ed, who had voted to stay at their crash site, was hanging back, refusing to wade into the dark current to get to the waiting craft. Adam pulled on his arm, long past asking him nicely to move.

Four Wolves burst from the bushes behind them.

"Adam, jump!" I screamed.

He leaped onto the zodiac as the Wolves lunged at the man left behind. Everyone screamed—the people in the boats who had never seen anything like a Wolf, and poor old Ed, whose screams were abruptly cut off as the Wolves ripped him apart.

"Go! Go! Go!"

I revved the engine on my watercraft. Two of the Wolves turned toward us and tensed their haunches to leap.

They landed less than a meter away as my zodiac caught the current and sputtered out onto the deep sea channel.

CHAPTER 13

CALEB

The Wolves dragged themselves back onto shore, glaring at us and shaking the water from their gray hides. They returned to what was left of their meal and I pivoted to face the terrified people in my boat. Carmen and Fernando were in the front, and two men whose names I'd forgotten were flattened against the bottom of the boat.

Fernando edged around the side toward me. "I don't like this, crossing by day."

I snorted and gestured back to the receding shoreline. "Do you want to go back?"

The men in the bottom of the boat were wide-eyed. One of them said in a tiny voice, "We don't want to go back."

The zodiac's engine growled under the strain of the over-full cargo. Kintan's boat was well ahead of mine, and Adam's flanked me on the right.

"We're not going back," I said. "And we need to be quiet. Sound travels well over water. Probably under it, too."

Wires were hung haphazardly around the edge of the zodiac, and a sat trans blinked its strobe hanging on a length of rope beneath us. I squinted up at the sun. *Too bright. They might not even see it. And if they do, they might not remember what it means.*

Kintan's boat was halfway across the channel when I got my answer.

A huge tail flipped up from the depths, capsizing his craft. Kintan, Nirah, and three other people spilled into the water.

Adam veered his zodiac toward the upside-down boat and I aimed mine slightly downstream. When the water settled, I saw three figures gripping the edge of the capsized boat. *Must have lost the lightning stick, or they'd be electrocuted by now.*

"Go get the zodiac!" I yelled to Adam. "I'm looking for two more!"

A giant shadow darkened the water beneath my boat. About ten meters away, a figure slapped and clawed at the surface. Another ten meters downstream, the water churned with the other person's frantic attempt to stay afloat. I aimed the zodiac between them.

Scat, no.

The upstream figure was Nirah. Downstream was Kintan.

Oh, no. Don't make me choose. But I had only a moment to decide. If I hesitated, we would lose them both.

I aimed the boat toward Nirah.

"Haul up the lightning stick and turn off the power," I screamed to Fernando. "The wires!" They were electrified to ward off a 'saur. If she touched them, she was fried.

Kintan splashed and gurgled in my view, getting farther away as I eased the zodiac toward Nirah.

"Pull her in, fast!"

Fernando hauled Nirah from the water. She flopped into the bottom of the boat, retching and gagging.

I'm coming, Kintan.

I gunned the engine, looking up to where Kintan struggled to swim. He wasn't there.

Too late, too late.

He reappeared with a splash, clawing at the water.

Stay up, buddy. I'm coming.

The huge shadow appeared under his struggling form. A giant triangular mouth opened from below, snapping its jaws to swallow Kintan whole. It sucked in a vortex of water when it sank beneath the surface.

I slammed the zodiac to the right, feeling the water disappear out from under the left side of the boat, into the hole where my friend just disappeared. Water pounded in to fill the hole as the 'saur dropped back into the depths.

"Kintan!" I screamed. But it was far too late.

Adam got the capsized zodiac right side up, and the three survivors loaded into it. A few shouted instructions, and one of them took the engine, aiming for the far shore. Three boats in parallel, we raced for land.

Fernando watched the sea behind us, wide-eyed over the edge of the boat.

Twenty meters. Ten.

Five.

We ran the boats right up onto shore and bailed out, sprinting up the rocky edge. Fernando carried Nirah, who was still coughing up seawater. When the shore turned to pine needles, we collapsed together, panting. Most of the Transport Eight survivors were too shocked to cry, but two of them were weeping in huge, gasping sobs.

"We can't stay here." I struggled to my feet and peered up and down the length of the pines as far as I could see.

"Are there things like that over here?" Carmen whispered.

I nodded. "We didn't see anything on this side before we crossed, but there could be. We need to get high into the mountains before it gets too dark to travel."

No one needed any further urging. We left the zodiacs at the water's edge and dragged ourselves onto the rocky slopes.

★ ★ ★

We risked a fire that night, camped on a ledge high above the pines below. There wasn't much to burn, and I hated the idea that we were a beacon to anything that might prowl the hills here, but the Eight crew were too terrified to survive a night in the total darkness of the mountain.

"Nothing big enough to hurt us up here," I murmured as everyone clustered around the little blaze. "We're safe in the mountains, and you never have to go down there again."

No one wanted to eat, but I forced everyone to chew on meat strips. We had filled our four canteens from a stream near the bottom of the hill, and took turns sipping from them.

"It's just a couple days walking now," I said.

You sound stupid. They're not children; you don't have to soothe them like babies. But I did. They looked at me with naked terror, especially the four people who had flipped over in the zodiac.

Nirah was sitting away from the fire propped up against a rock. I took a canteen and meat strip over to her.

She stared straight ahead toward the little flame. "Did you come to tell me you were right?"

I held out the canteen. "Of course not."

The fire popped and snapped.

"You should. You were. You know this place better than I do. I should have listened."

The rock was cool on my back as I flopped down next to her. "Yes. But I should have insisted. I knew what the danger was, and I still watched those people go out onto that field."

She sipped from the canteen. "What were those things?"

Even now the click echoed in my head. "Something I never thought I'd have to see again. We call them Wolves because they hunt in packs. When you hear that clicking noise, it means someone is about to die." I held out a meat stick, but Nirah waved it off.

"Three years I kept them alive. Kim and Laran. And Ed, too." She glanced over at me. "You pulled me out of that water first. It cost Kintan his life."

My stomach turned over, the meat strip sour in my mouth.

"I know."

"You had to choose." She shook her head. "Not something I would wish on the most seasoned captain."

Oh, Kintan. He had a pregnant wife back at Carthage. I would have to tell her. *Tell her I chose to rescue Nirah instead of Kintan.*

Nirah sighed. "I underestimated you and it cost four people's lives. I will not do it again. Please, Caleb. Please get the rest of my people back safely."

The stars shone so brightly out here in the darkness. One of the glittering lights was Horizon Alpha, with a dozen people on it depending on us to rescue them. Nirah was their only hope. I'd sacrificed my friend Kintan, who had been with me since the journey to Transport Seventeen, for the chance to save those people in the sky.

I whispered to the stars, "I will."

CHAPTER 14

CALEB

We traveled across the mountains for five days. The happy group that had clustered to hear each other's stories in the smelly hold of Transport Eight were somber now, eyes on the rocks in front of them. There was no lively chatter, no stories or questions. Only climbing and descending, up one side and down the other. The paint marks were still visible and we followed our trail back toward Carthage.

"Not much farther now," I said, encouraging each little group of climbers. "We might make it back tonight if we really push."

We took a break at noon to eat and rest. Some of the packs had been on the capsized zodiac, but we had enough to comfortably complete our journey, even if we had to camp one more night.

Carmen and Fernando were sitting near the edge of the drop off. The land sloped down behind them out of sight. When I called for everyone to start moving, we all stood and grabbed our packs. As usual, I fell into the back of the line, alert for anything behind us. Nothing bigger than a rock-hopper up here. A sigh escaped my lips. *We're close. We're not going to lose anyone else.*

Carmen stumbled over a large rock, dislodging it. From beneath it, a small snake whipped out at her leg. She screamed and jumped to the side.

Fernando grabbed for her arm, but he was too slow. She slid down the steep ravine out of sight.

"Carmen!" he screamed, lunging for the edge.

I pulled him back, dropping to my knees to peer over.

She was hanging onto a large stone, and when she turned to look up at us, her face was scraped all over one side.

"Hang on!" I yelled to her. "I'm coming down to get you!"

We didn't have much rope, another casualty of the channel crossing. Adam tossed me a small coil and I tied a large loop in one end, handing the other to Fernando. "I'm going to get her into this side, and you pull her up, okay?"

He nodded, and I lowered myself over the edge.

I had climbed steeper and more challenging ledges. There was a wide crack with good handholds and I reached her in no time. I wedged my feet into the crack and shoved the rope over to her with one hand.

"You're going to have to let go with one hand and get this around you. Fernando will pull you up." I eased myself down another meter and grabbed her leg. "Put your foot here. There's a good hold."

With a shaking hand she managed to flop the loop of rope around one shoulder. As soon as it was under her armpit, Fernando pulled it taut.

"Go slow and hold the rope," I cautioned. "Don't try to climb. Let him do the pulling. You just steady your feet and hang onto the rope."

Fernando began to pull her up. She scrambled her feet against the rocky edge and I jerked away from the debris.

Her foot slipped just as I reached out to steady her. She kicked me in the face and my hands grasped empty air as my neck whipped backwards.

I tumbled down the slope, skidding to a stop about twenty

meters down from where Carmen was being pulled over the edge by her brother.

Something sharp pierced my skin. I pulled away from the sting, and felt a slash down my left arm.

The wound only hurt for a moment before the pain drained away into nothing. A heavy calm flooded into me. I felt like I was being dragged under water, deeper and deeper into the dark, slow current. My eyes wandered to the side where I noticed a small 'saur lolling next to me, caught in the same poison wicked thorns that held me fast.

Tired. Comfortable.

It didn't hurt. It was nice here. There was shouting from far away, but the warm sun made my eyelids so heavy. I smiled and sighed, and drifted into hazy darkness.

CHAPTER 15

SHIRO

I was on guard duty on the north edge when I saw the first glimpse of the return of our party.

"I see them!" I shouted into my sat trans, and got a confirmation from the rest of the guys stationed around the edges of our valley.

From my vantage point in the lowest pass, I couldn't make out any individuals as they came over the crest of another pass just outside our protective wall. We had been in contact with the group for two days now, and knew they'd been successful in finding Nirah and eleven other survivors. We also knew that Kintan had been lost in the return crossing. Mayor Borin had told Kintan's wife, and we added his name to the wall where we kept the long list of those who had fallen to this planet's many dangers.

The group was straggled out in a long line with one bulky figure in the front. It took me a minute to figure out what looked so odd about the shape.

He was carrying a body.

"Carthage Valley, this is Shiro Yamoto. Someone's in trouble out there. I'm heading out." I didn't wait for a response before starting my descent over our protective mountainside.

Whoever it is, they're still alive. No one would be carrying a dead body back to Carthage, no matter who it was. We had never been a culture that was sentimental about body care. On Horizon, the dead were processed into fertilizer for our algae tanks and water, our most precious resource. On Ceti, we didn't usually have a body left to consider.

I scrambled down the rocks as fast as I could, heading for the figure. Whoever it was, he looked tired. His steps were shuffling and the limp form over his shoulder dangled awkwardly.

As he got closer I could tell it was Fernando.

And he was carrying Caleb.

All thoughts of caution forgotten, I bolted across the hills.

"What happened?" I was shouting as I approached and Fernando barely looked up, focusing on each labored step. The rest of the group was quite a ways behind him, not near enough for me to make out anyone's face.

Fernando panted, moving as fast as he could. When I got to him I reached for Caleb.

"Let me take him. What happened?"

But Fernando wouldn't let me have my best friend.

"Thorns," he muttered. "Poison."

I could barely tell that the limp Caleb was still breathing, lolling over the big man's shoulder with arms dangling down his back. "Let me take him, buddy. You're exhausted."

He shook his head. "Almost there."

There was no way he'd make the final climb over our protective ring of mountains. We had rigged a few pitons and ropes in preparation for this group's return, but it was a steep climb. He couldn't do it alone. I called into my sat trans again.

"Carthage base, we have a man down. Send all available to Lookout Three, and bring whatever rope you can."

By the time we reached the base of the final ascent, three of our guys were halfway down, trailing the knotted rope we made from the plants that grew around our lake. Fernando finally let Caleb down off his shoulder and we wrapped the ropes around his chest under his arms and between his legs making the safest quick harness we could. It wouldn't be pretty hauling him up the rocky slope.

"Come on, Caleb," I whispered to his still, slack form. "You're home. Just gotta make it in to your mom."

His chest was rising and falling slowly, a long string of drool hanging from his lower lip. His eyes were open and staring, pupils huge in the late afternoon sun.

"All right, I'll steady him as we go. Pull!"

The guys higher on the hill pulled on the ropes and I tried to keep Caleb's head from bouncing into anything too hard. There was no way to avoid tearing up the back of his shirt on the rocks as we dragged him higher and higher up the mountainside.

With a shower of stones, Josh slid in next to me about halfway up.

"What happened to him?" His eyes were wild as he grabbed for his brother's arm.

"Fernando said it was those thorns." I gestured down the hill. "Those poison ones that make the 'saurs just sit there drooling until they die."

Josh pulled Caleb's shoulder and I took the other side, supporting him as the ropes hauled his weight up the steep incline. We didn't talk any more as we climbed, focused on one hand up, one foot up, support Caleb's head, and repeat. After the better part of an hour, I could finally see over the edge. A crowd had gathered at the bottom of the valley.

"Should be easier on the way down. Come on, buddy. Stay with us." Caleb didn't respond to my words.

I looked back down the way we had come. Fernando was still collapsed at the bottom of the climb, and the rest of his party was straggling up to him. This wouldn't be an easy climb for any of them, but they would have to fend for themselves, at least until we got Caleb safely into the cave.

We worked our way down the shallower slope into the valley. Caleb's mom was waiting at the bottom, along with three more people and a pole-and-strap stretcher. We flopped Caleb onto it and I took one corner. Together we jogged across the valley, carrying my downed friend.

"It's the thorns," I panted to Caleb's mom as we ran. "The poison thorns."

She nodded, running alongside us with her hand on her son's wrist. "Narcotic." Her fingers pushed at several fresh puncture wounds on Caleb's arms. "So many."

We finally got him into the infirmary where the other doctor was waiting, along with three of the older kids who were starting their medical training. They had hung curtains around the beds we had built and one of the kids tried to shut me out when they laid Caleb on the bed.

"No way." I shoved the kid aside and reached for Caleb.

"Shiro, please," Dr. Wilde said. "We need room here."

I backed away at the tone of Caleb's mom's voice. They pulled the curtain shut and I collapsed, shaking, to the floor of the cave.

They worked on Caleb all night. I stayed on the floor of the cave just outside the infirmary, waiting for news. I must have drifted off to sleep because some time later I was roused by the smell of cooked meat and a soft voice.

"Shiro? I brought you some food."

The voice. *I must be dreaming.*

"Shiro?"

I opened my eyes to a vision.

Carmen Orellana. Setting a plate of hot food down next to me.

I bolted up from the floor. Carmen was grinning, tears in her eyes. She threw her arms around me and I buried my nose in her hair, squeezing her until she must have been unable to breathe. She was so skinny. She pulled away and stood at arm's length, the same old smile I had dreamed about for three long years on her beautiful face.

"You're here. You're alive." My words sounded stupid even to me, but Carmen didn't seem to mind.

"I knew you were alive somewhere," she whispered. "I knew it. Every night, all these years, I knew you had to be here and I had to find you."

My eyes lowered, shame burning at my lack of faith. I never imagined she could still be alive out there. Even after we found the last batch of survivors, it never occurred to me that we might find another transport full of people, and she might be in it.

We had never been much on pretense, me and Carmen. "I had given up," I told her. "We lost so many. I never thought I'd see you again."

She melted back into my arms and we stood there forever. Her hair smelled like sweat and her bony shoulders felt like a bag of sticks, but I breathed in the scent of her and felt joy seeping in with each breath.

"Shiro?" A voice from the infirmary made me whip my head around. Caleb's mom was standing there, dark circles under her eyes.

"What is it?" My mouth was dry and I spat the words around a cotton tongue. "Is he . . . ?" I couldn't finish it.

She gave a tired smile. "He's alive. Not awake yet. Maybe won't be awake for a while. Do you want to come see him?"

I took Carmen's hand and we followed Dr. Wilde into the cave room.

We didn't have all the medical equipment we should have if the Horizon evacuation hadn't been such a mess, but we had a heart monitor, and its regular beep reassured me as I approached my best friend.

He was deathly pale, lying under a warm blanket. His eyes were still open and looked wet. There was a breathing tube disappearing into his mouth, and a bag on the machine pushed air into his lungs, making his chest rise and fall under the cover. Every few seconds his whole body would twitch and the green line on the heart monitor would jump.

"What's wrong with him?" I asked, not taking my eyes off him. "When's he gonna wake up?"

Dr. Wilde sat on the bed next to her son and took his hand. "I'm not really sure. We don't know a lot about the toxin, and we don't have a specific antidote. He was so lucky to make it here in time. He stopped breathing on his own just a few minutes after we got him in here." A tear dripped onto her cheek, quickly brushed away. "If Fernando hadn't moved as fast as he did . . ."

"But he did," I interrupted. "He got Caleb here in time."

She nodded. "I hope so. We got all the thorns out of him, so now we just have to hope that when the narcotic wears off he'll start breathing on his own."

Hope. She was *hoping* he'd wake up. She wasn't sure.

"How long do you think it will take?"

She didn't know. "I hope not too long."

We held a council meeting that night in the room we used as an armory. Mayor Borin had added Nirah to the official council, and she sat between him and Don Rand, holding a mug of something hot. She looked awful, too. Skinny like Carmen. Wherever they had found themselves hiding this past three years, there obviously hadn't been enough food.

Mayor Borin called the meeting to order. "Welcome, Nirah, to Carthage Valley. We're so glad you and your group have joined us."

Nirah smiled. "And we're certainly glad to be here." She looked around at our little group. "Thank you for risking the lives of your people to come and find us."

The Mayor sighed. "As much as we'd like to let you rest and get acclimated, we have important business to discuss."

The mug Nirah was holding gave off a strong smell of herbs, some kind of tea. She wrapped her hands tightly around it and lowered it into her lap. "I know. Caleb told me along the way.

Captain's still up there." She gestured toward the ceiling.

"And my daughter," Don added.

We were all perched on crates around a table brought from one of the old transports.

Nirah pulled a pile of paper from her pocket. "So is this right, then? We have one non-working shuttle here that you pulled half the wiring and one engine out of to fix the one you wrecked on your last flight?"

I scowled. "We didn't wreck it. We left it and when we got back to it, the 'saurs had wrecked it."

She shook her head. "Whatever. It's too far to salvage. And I can't fix a shuttle with no parts."

Don grabbed at one of the papers. "There are four transports and two other non-working shuttles back at our old base. And the tank still runs."

Nirah peered at him. "How far?"

"About four hours by tank," I said.

She looked around the table at our hopeful faces. "You realize this is basically impossible, right? I know you risked your lives to find us, and I'm forever grateful for that." She shook her head. "But our ships weren't made for this planet. You're asking me to rewrite the laws of physics."

Mayor Borin sighed. "I know. I've been thinking about it night and day since we found out our people were still alive up there. I don't have an answer, and if you can't do it, we're still so happy to have found you and brought you home."

Nirah snorted at the word. "It's hardly home, is it? But it's the best we're going to do. Hope the other Horizon ships find a warmer welcome, wherever they are." She grabbed the paper back from Don and peered at it, muttering, "Horizon, Horizon." After a few moments she began scribbling on it, mumbling to herself. "It's four hundred kilometers straight up. If I use the transport's engine? We'd get the power but it would be too heavy." The tip of her tongue stuck out the side of her mouth as she worked. "We need lift to get into low orbit."

Sara looked over Nirah's shoulder. "Back on earth, they used to shoot their shuttles straight up. Controlled explosion in the booster rockets to get into orbit, and the shuttle would separate from the booster once it got high enough."

Nirah nodded. "Ours weren't meant to launch that way, but . . ." She trailed off, tapping the pencil against her lips. "How soon can we leave to go get parts?"

No one answered for a long moment. *What would Caleb say?* My hands slapped on the tabletop. "Tomorrow morning."

Murmurs filled the room until Mayor Borin motioned for silence. "We can put a party together as soon as you have a list of the parts they'll need to acquire."

"I'll write the list on the way," Nirah said. "I'm not sure what we'll need until I get over that wall and see what's left of the shuttle we have."

"Don can . . ." Mayor Borin began, but Nirah cut him off.

"Yes, Don can. And so can I, but better. You risked a lot of lives because you know I'm the only one who has a hope of getting us up to Horizon again. So if you think I'm going to sit in this cave while someone else tries to do my job, you can just forget that right now."

Sara caught my eye and we shared a grin.

Nirah continued, "And while we're out there, you can figure out a plan for when the Flood comes."

We all looked blank, and she sighed. Sara's expression went from eager to horrified as Nirah told us about the hundreds of thousands of tiny 'saurs that had flooded her valley every year since they landed.

"But we don't get them here," I protested. "We never saw them at Eden."

"Your base was southwest of here, right? They must head east once they get to the jungle. Or spread out so much that they're not a threat to anything big. But I'd be shocked if they didn't come through these mountains. And I'm not going anywhere until I know my people are going to be safe when they do." Her jaw was set, eyes boring into the mayor's.

He spread his hands on the table. "We'll deal with it if it

happens. The important thing now is to get our people down from that ship."

Nirah's eyes were fire. "If it happens, there won't be time to 'deal with it.' They'll pour through this valley and nothing will survive. You can hide in these caves and think they won't find you, but there's thousands and thousands, and they'll kill every living thing they see. There needs to be a plan. We evacuate back to your old base where they didn't come." She stood up and looked around the room. "I know you don't believe me. But I believed you. I trusted Caleb when he showed up talking about dinosaurs and Birdmen, and I brought my people here thinking we would be safer. I can fix your shuttle. It will fly. But if there's no plan to survive the Flood here in this valley by the time it's done, I'm using it to fly my people right back up to our old transport. There isn't room for everyone there, but I won't be around to watch you die."

CHAPTER 16

CAPTAIN'S PERSONAL JOURNAL, YEAR TWO, DAY 38.

We lost Barton today.

Once again, it was my fault. Bethany had an idea that would allow us to interrupt the sat trans signal from the surface in a pattern. We could program a repeating interruption in Morse Code. I think it's next to impossible that anyone will ever notice that tiny disruption and make out that it's a repeating code, but there's nothing to be gained by dashing her hopes. She thought it could work, and that when they finally do realize we're here, we'll be able to communicate in code. It still won't allow them to come rescue us, but all of us have family or friends at Eden Base. The idea of communicating with them in any way seemed to revitalize everyone's flagging spirits, so we planned the spacewalk to reach the receiver array and attach her disruptor module.

I should have realized that Barton wasn't up to the task. General Singh was his brother-in-law, and Barton took the news of his death pretty hard. Some days I wish we couldn't hear them on the trans. No one should hear a man get bitten in half by a dinosaur. But he assured me he was all right, and he was the only crewmember besides me to have any spacewalking experience. It's dangerous to leave the ship, and we only did it for critical repairs.

It was a stupid mistake. We have grave concerns about all the airlocks since so many of the Horizon systems have failed since the fire. Leaving our pressurized cylinder for the central axis or either of the other depressurized wrecked tubes is hugely dangerous. If the airlocks fail to hold, our cylinder could depressurize as well. Even if everyone got into an exposure suit in time, we would last a day or two at most before the oxygen scrubbers gave out and we suffocated in the helmets.

The spacewalk started out fine. The double airlocks leading out of Tube Three both worked and we floated free down the long axis of the ship, bouncing off the walls as we reoriented ourselves to zero gravity. Junk floated everywhere . . . dust and debris that would ordinarily sit on floors and shelves was untethered by gravity, bobbing around in clouds of detritus. The emergency lights were still on, throwing our shadows onto the walls.

Because we were concerned about opening an external airlock anywhere near our life support systems, we decided to traverse the entire axis up to Tube One, and exit the ship through the hole that was blown open on the day we entered orbit. We would have to be careful of sharp edges on the way in and out, and would begin to tether ourselves to the ship before we stepped outside.

Three internal airlocks separated us from Tube One, failsafes that had held so far. We got into our exposure suits and ran an extensive buddy check, making sure our suits were functioning before leaving the first lock. It shut behind us, and we proceeded through the next two, holding in the small chambers between each side of the lock and praying they would close behind us and open in front of us like they were supposed to. They did, and we eventually made it to the burned-out hull of Tube One. I had the disruptor module, a small metal box, attached to my left thigh with a tether. Sliding links on my belt would allow me to attach myself to the ship as I worked my way along, unclipping from one tether after securely clipping in to the next. Redundancy is key to survival in space.

I went out first, pushing off from what had been the inner wall of one of the dining halls. Most of the tables and chairs had long since floated out the hole, but I pushed past utensils and plates, pots and pans as I aimed for the center. My tether was attached on the inside and would stop my forward motion, allowing me to swing past the jagged edge and land on the external surface of the ship. My heart was pounding in my ears as I sailed through the hole and into the bright light of Ceti's sun. I held the tether, controlling my stop so I wouldn't jerk the line, and swung over to grab onto one of the many large rounded handholds all over the outside of the ship. I clipped a second line to the handhold and attached the first long tether to the hold as well, so I could use it to re-enter the ship once the job was done. It was a long way around the cylinder to the communication array, and I reminded myself not to hurry.

The helmet of my suit allowed no peripheral vision. I only saw Barton's shadow as he emerged from the ship, right in the center of the hole, away from the sharp edge as planned. He didn't hold his tether and it jerked him to a stop, swinging him over toward me. I grabbed his hand as he approached and helped him clip onto the handhold, attaching his long interior tether to mine. We made another buddy check, and proceeded across the ship's exterior, handhold to handhold, clipping on and off as we went. We were very careful. It took almost three hours to reach the array. Installing the module to Bethany's instruction took another hour. Simple jobs take forever when your tools float away if you let them go. Every screwdriver and set of pliers were velcroed to our suits. The helmet comms worked, and we were able to talk to Bethany, who waited back in Tube Three. But out here it was just Barton and me, watching sunrise and sunset every two hours as we orbited the planet. I couldn't even be sure I had installed it correctly, but I checked everything I could check before we began the three-hour journey back to the hole that would lead us inside.

We finally reached the entrance and I grabbed the tethers

we had attached hours before. I handed one to Barton, making sure it was securely fastened to his belt before I let go of it. Mine clipped onto my belt and Barton nodded to me. I was in charge of the mission, first out and last in. So I saw it happen right before my eyes.

Looking back on it, I assume that when he emerged from the ship and the belt jerked him to a halt when we first exited, the ancient metal must have been weakened. Our plan was to step free of the ship, pushing out past the edge, and haul hand over hand back inside.

He pushed off, floating away from me. He held onto his tether, preparing to pull himself back in.

I saw his face the moment he realized his interior connection had failed, and the line he was pulling was just reeling out toward him, not pulling him in. He was no longer attached to the exterior handhold, nor to me. And the line he was holding was attached to nothing but his belt.

I tried. Stupidly, I jumped toward him, hoping to grab the loose end of his tether before he floated out of range. I lunged toward him, seeing the panic in his eyes as I relied on my tether to keep me from floating free as well.

Back before Horizon fell apart, we trained for this kind of emergency. Our suits had small jet packs that were supposed to help us return to the ship if this unthinkable accident happened and we found ourselves untethered and floating free in space. As I flew through the vacuum toward him, I could see him trying to engage his pack. I could see when it ignited, sparked, and sputtered into stillness.

But I was almost there. His line was reeling out in front of me and I reached out to grab it.

My line jerked on my belt, halting my movement. My fingers grasped for Barton's line, the tips of my glove tapping the bent carabiner that was supposed to attach him to the ship's interior. It spun out of my grasp.

Meter by meter, I watched him float away.

I could have unclipped myself and trusted my jet pack to

ignite, hoping I could reach his line and somehow get us turned around and back to the ship. But his had failed. And I wasn't brave enough. I hung there in space reaching out toward my fellow crewman as he drifted off into the blinding crescent of a Tau Ceti sunset.

CHAPTER 17

SHIRO

I hated leaving Caleb, but there was no time to waste. We set a crew to digging out our "front door," the cave that collapsed when we last set foot out into the jungle. Our tank sat outside that entrance, as did our derelict shuttle. Nirah, Don, Fernando, Adam, and I were all heading out in the morning once the path was cleared enough for us to crawl through. We would take the tank back to our old Eden Base and salvage whatever Nirah needed to get the shuttle flying again with enough power to leave Ceti's gravity and get into orbit to rendezvous with Horizon Alpha. Carmen didn't want me to go. She hung on my arm as I stood over Caleb's bed, listening to the rhythmic rise and fall of the ventilator. He was twitching more than yesterday. Was that a good sign or a bad one? No one seemed to know.

I perched on the edge of the bed. "Hey, buddy. I'm heading out in the morning." His mom had told me that Caleb might be able to hear what was going on around him, even if he couldn't respond. "Nirah's coming out with me and we're going to get that shuttle working. She thinks it will take us a week to get everything we need and get back here. Plenty of time to fix the shuttle and go get your dad."

Nothing from Caleb.

He looked so young lying there. I remembered his first mission, him bouncing in the seat in front of me next to Jack. Just a kid. I remembered how he'd hung back from the group when the General led them away from me after the crash and the accident. Caleb was the last one I could see as I crawled out onto a tree hanging over a river where I knew I was going to die. He looked like that kid again now, staring sightlessly into space. His cheeks were getting hollow. How much longer could he go without waking up to eat something? Would his mom put in some kind of feeding tube to keep him alive?

"So anyway," I said, "I'll be back in a week. We'll get the shuttle fixed and go get your dad and all the stuff we need. So you better . . . you know. Wake up. So you're awake when your dad gets back."

Carmen's fingers brushed my cheek and I realized I was crying.

Caleb had come back for me all those months ago, found me where I lay on the riverbank, broken and battered. Jack was dead. Brent was dead. The General was dead. But Caleb found me.

I gripped his hand now, willing him to wake up. He twitched but did not awaken.

"Okay, buddy. I'll see you real soon."

We left the sound of the beeping heart monitor and let the curtain fall behind us.

The tank roared to life on the third attempt to start it.

One hurdle down. I'd been worried it might not run since we'd abandoned it out here after the last mission. Without the tank we'd have no way to get the parts from Eden Base back here to the shuttle. But finally, for the first time, something seemed to be going right.

Five of us crammed into the close quarters and Adam drove us into the jungle. There were a couple of tiny windows on each side, thick, bulletproof glass smudged with the dirt of neglect. I watched the trees roll by as we growled along. My leg started to cramp and I massaged the thigh where the broken bone that almost killed me hadn't healed quite straight.

I had expected Nirah to have her face pressed against the glass, like Caleb had on his first flight into the jungle. That seemed like forever ago. But her nose was buried in the notes on her trans. She had spent all day yesterday crawling around our broken shuttle, muttering to herself and sighing. At the end of the day she had compiled a list of the parts we'd need to salvage from the transports back at our abandoned base. She was confident she could get the shuttle flying again if we could get everything we needed.

I rubbed at the spot on my leg that still pained me when I overdid it. A storm was coming, probably later tonight. The healed fracture didn't lie about the weather.

The darkness of the forest floor shadowed the little windows. We figured about four hours to get to Base. That would leave some daylight left to get ourselves situated inside whichever transport looked the most promising. We could do a lot of the salvage work from inside the ships, which would obviously be a whole lot safer. But some of the parts we needed weren't accessible from inside. So we'd either have to rig a lighting system and work at night, risking the warm, bright beacon that would provide for any big hungry 'saur in the area, or work by day and risk every single carnivore in the forest. Adam was nominally in charge of this mission and would have to make the call when we got there.

The interior of the tank smelled like mold and sweat. We rolled along all morning and into the heat of afternoon, finally halting on the edge of the forest just outside the clearing that had been our home for three long years. I popped the hatch and waited, listening to the sounds of the jungle. Little 'saurs were shrieking all around—a good sign. Fresh air flooded in, the familiar scent of wet dirt and growing things. I was first out the top, leading with my rifle.

A quick perimeter scan showed nothing bigger than a human.

Across a long expanse of open field sat the remains of our base. Six transports sat in a rough circle, rusting and dented. The remains of our electric fence dangled all around the ships, creaking against the hulls in a slight, hot wind. A few of the wire sections were intact, but most had already fallen. *Didn't take the 'saurs long to figure out the power went down.* I shuddered to think how close our colony had come to still being inside that fence when the electricity ran out.

A few little 'saurs hopped around the transports, and a small herd of tank-sized grazers browsed the field between our tank and the ships. All good signs that no big predators were hunting nearby. No guarantees, of course. Most of the best hunters were successful because the herd never saw them coming.

I waited a few more minutes, binoculars pressed to my face. Finally I crawled back down into the hull.

"Looks all right. All the transports look more or less intact from here. Let's just get to the closest one and get inside."

Adam nodded and the tank grumbled forward into the field. The 'saurs scattered around us, hopping and lumbering out of our way.

We pulled up right next to the closest ship and opened the hatch again. I scuttled out the top and jumped down, staying low as I moved to the smallest hatch on the transport. My heart was pounding and a familiar electricity zipped through my nerves. The transport hatch was stuck shut and I had to brace a foot on the wall to tug it open. The noise it made drove needles into my spine.

I guess any 'saur around knows we're here.

"Come on, guys, Get inside."

The rest of the group poured out of the tank and dashed into the transport. I squealed the door shut behind us and we all gave a sigh.

There wasn't much left inside the ship. We'd taken everything we thought might be useful when we made the move to Carthage.

It would be an uncomfortable week in the old ship, but we had work to do. The sooner we started, the sooner we'd get back to our valley.

Nirah was already heading up to the cockpit, trans list in hand. "Come on and help me. We can start with this one and hope what I need is all here."

I started to follow her but was stopped by Adam's voice. He was standing at one of the windows on the other side of the shuttle facing into the protected ring we had called home. "Um, guys? Might want to check this out."

We joined him at the window, rubbing at the grimy surface to see out.

"What? I don't see . . ." I trailed off when I spotted it.

Nestled on the other side of the circle, under the wing of the transport where I'd spent three long years, was a rough nest made of logs, sticks, and some of the debris we'd left behind. Inside the nest were three huge eggs.

I raised my sat trans, intending to take a picture to send to Sara. She would know what they were.

But I didn't have to ask. The ground rumbled beneath our feet, making dust sift down from the ceiling. The herd of grazers lumbered away from the outside of the circle.

Through the broken wires on the east side of our base, a Rex pounded into the clearing.

"It's going to eat the eggs," Fernando said.

It didn't eat the eggs.

It was carrying a small tree in its mouth, which it deposited next to the nest. The huge nose shoved the tree into place, shoring up the edge of the nest. We all held our breaths as the Rex sniffed each egg, turning them with its enormous face.

Her enormous face.

She curled herself around the nest, tail wrapped around the sides, and with a giant crash that wobbled the side of the transport, lay down to guard her eggs.

CHAPTER 18

SHIRO

"Well."

Nirah's single word summed up the helplessness we all felt.

"Can we kill it?" Don stared out the window at the Rex, his breath fogging up the thick glass.

I shook my head. "We've never found anything that will kill a Rex. Bullets just bounce off." I turned to Nirah, who was also glued to the window. "How much of the stuff we need can be accessed from inside the transport?"

She tore her gaze away from the Rex on her nest and considered my question. "There's a lot we should be able to get to, but it won't be quiet. That thing will know something's going on in here. Can it get in?"

I remembered another transport. An open door and the long arm of a Rex, dragging my friend Jack to his death. "She could reach in if the door were open."

"So we don't open the door. Ever." Fernando towered over Don, peering over the top of his head.

Nirah switched her trans on, checking her notes. "We can't do it all from inside. Sooner or later we have to get outside to the engine. You guys did a number on that shuttle."

The sun was slanting in the windows, and the Rex's shadow loomed over our base. I pulled out my trans and opened the channel, returning to my first intention. "Carthage Base, this is Away Team. We have a situation. We need Sara."

I repeated the call a couple of times until a voice came on the line. It was choppier than usual, and I cursed the accident that prevented our satellites from launching when we arrived here on Horizon. The ship in its orbit was our main communication link. The other satellites' orbits were erratic, and neither was currently in range.

"Shiro? What's going on?" Sara's words were clipped and broken up.

I got right to the point. "There's a Rex nest in the middle of Base. One female guarding it. Eggs are big, about a meter in diameter."

She made a sharp intake of breath. "You need to stay far away, and downwind. She can't know you're there."

"She already does, I'm sure," I answered, glancing out the window. The Rex hadn't moved, but her black eye was focused in our direction. "She must have heard the tank. We're inside Transport Nine, and Nirah says we can get some of what we need from inside. But we have to work outside sooner or later. So how long 'till the eggs hatch? And how long 'till they leave?"

The answer returned. "I have no idea. Depends how long they've already been incubating. If I had to guess, it sounds like they could hatch anytime. But we don't know how long they stay at a nest." She paused a moment. "Just one adult?"

"So far."

Adam spoke up from the front of the shuttle where he was setting up a rudimentary indoor camp with the provisions we'd brought. "Can we move the eggs while she's gone? Would she stay where the eggs are?"

"Or crush them?" Don suggested.

"Guys, I don't know." Sara sounded dejected. She knew we relied on her knowledge. "It's possible she'd bring the eggs back to the nest. And it's also possible that if you crushed the eggs, she'd go completely crazy and destroy everything in that base."

I'd seen what little 'saurs did when their eggs were squashed. No way did I want to see a Rex that angry. But we couldn't just sit and wait. Nirah was certain The Flood was coming and was determined to have the shuttle flying by then as a last-ditch effort to save her people. Her impatience was contagious, and I tapped my foot, pacing around with the sat trans.

"Okay," I said. "We'll do what we can inside and see what we can figure out. If you have any ideas, let us know. And how's Caleb? Has he woken up yet?"

"You guys be—don't—Caleb is—can't . . ." The sat trans connection went dead.

"Scat. Lost her." I tried to reopen the line, but there was no signal. No satellite.

I glanced up toward the ceiling, as if to look through the steel and up to the sky where Horizon should have been connecting our signal. "Don, I'm not getting out."

He grabbed my trans and ran his fingers over the screen, frowning. "It's working all right. But not seeing the satellite. Who else has a trans?"

Adam turned his on and scowled at the screen. "No signal here either."

No signal. It shouldn't have panicked me. We'd intermittently lost connection before when weather or tree cover blocked us from Horizon's satellite arrays. We had traveled out of range on many occasions. But the sky was clear, and the ship should have been overhead. Neither of the other satellites were currently in range, but Horizon should have been near enough to use for another couple of months before its orbit took it out of range for the winter season.

"Could Horizon be off course?" I wondered.

Nirah shrugged. "Could be. Or could be damaged. All kinds of meteoroids showering a planet all the time. Something could have knocked out the array. Or something gone wrong on the inside."

We didn't have to speculate further on that. There were so many things that could go wrong on a damaged interstellar spacecraft.

"Will they realize we're down?"

"Of course. They won't be able to hear us because we're not transmitting." Nirah sighed. "The question is, can they fix it?"

And what would we do if they couldn't? If we got the shuttle running and figured out how to get it into orbit, would anyone be waiting to meet us? This was supposed to be a rescue mission. Was there anyone up there to rescue?

Outside the window the Rex shifted, snuggling closer around her eggs. Caleb's dad was up there. Caleb had risked his life in an attempt to save my father from the wreck of Transport Seventeen. He'd risked his life again to save mine when I'd shut down on the way back. I owed Caleb everything, and it was time to start paying that debt.

I stuffed the useless trans into my pack. "All right. We'll do what we can from inside. Let's get started."

CHAPTER 19

CALEB

The first thing I became aware of was an echoing voice in my head. I couldn't make out any of the words, but it pounded between my ears, growing louder and more insistent with every heartbeat. When I couldn't ignore it any longer, I opened my left eye a crack. The right one was glued shut. Light poured in and I slammed the left eye closed again, squinting against the drum beat inside my skull.

"Caleb? Caleb, honey, are you in there?"

That sounded like Mom.

"He's awake. I just saw him open his eyes."

That sounded like Josh.

I cracked the eye open again, peeking under a heavy eyelid. The right eye still wouldn't open and I reached up to rub it.

"There! He's moving! Caleb, buddy, you all right?"

My brother's face moved in to block the bright light, swimming in and out of focus. I tried to grunt a response but my throat felt like dry gravel and my mouth tasted like someone had used it to clean out the 'saur pen in the valley.

"Don't try to talk. Josh, get him some water. Just a little bit."

Yeah, that was Mom. A cup was forced between my lips and I sucked in a sip of cool water. It didn't want to go down my swollen throat and I coughed, snorting it out through my nose.

"Careful, buddy. Little sips. Let's prop you up and try again."

What on Ceti happened? My blurry vision clearly showed that I was in the infirmary at Carthage. *So we made it back.* Why was I here? Where was everyone else? And why did it feel like a Brachi was jumping on my head from the inside?

I sipped at the water until my throat opened up enough to gurgle out a word.

"Where?"

Josh jumped in. "You're home. Carthage. You got everybody back. You fell into one of those thorn bushes—the poison ones. Do you remember that? Fernando carried you all the way back."

I didn't remember that. *What do I remember? What's the last thing? Carmen. I remember Carmen.* My lips mumbled her name.

"She's fine." Mom was bustling around checking my vital signs. She was so obviously relieved that I was awake that I had to ask the next question.

"How long?"

Mom and Josh glanced at each other. "Total, a week. You were on the ventilator for the first five days. Last two you've been breathing on your own."

My stomach growled, a sick, acid feeling rumbling in my gut.

Mom laughed, her shoulders dropping from their hunched tension. "Good sign. Josh, you want to go get him something to eat? Bland. Maybe just a potato for now." My brother nodded and headed out of my sight.

I struggled to sit up, my back protesting the movement. When I moved, I got a whiff of my stench.

"I stink."

Mom grinned. "Yes, you do."

All my joints were sore, and my head still throbbed. Mom told me that I'd fallen into a thorn bush, the kind with the sedative that kept a 'saur happily stuck until it starved to death, or until a bigger 'saur came along and ate it.

"It works really well," she said, perched on the side of my bed with two fingers on my wrist to feel my pulse. "We've been trying to purify it to use as an anesthetic. It doesn't take much. And you got a wallop—ten punctures all over your backside. We don't have any kind of reversal agent, so we just had to keep you breathing until it wore off. We were hoping it *would* wear off."

She didn't have to say that. Or what would have happened to me if it hadn't.

"Nirah and the rest came in behind you," Mom continued. "She and a couple of the guys left to go down to the old base. They're getting parts, whatever Nirah needs to fix our shuttle." She stood up and frowned. "But for some reason we haven't been able to get a sat signal for a whole day now."

They left without me?

I swung my legs over the side of the bed and tried to push off the mattress. The heart monitor leads stuck to my chest beeped as they tore away from my skin. "I need to go."

Mom grabbed my shoulders just as my knees gave out from under me. She guided me back onto the bed instead of letting me crumple to the floor. "Easy, there. You're not going anywhere for a while. You've been on a ventilator for most of a week. Let's just take this one day at a time."

Josh came in with a small plate of cut up potato from our first crop of spuds. "Hey, Squirt. Here's dinner." He perched on the bed next to me and grabbed a cube of potato, holding it out toward my mouth.

I raised an eyebrow at him and grabbed the food. "You don't have to feed me. I'm okay."

He shrugged, smiling. "If you say so." He plopped the plate onto my lap.

The potato was dry and I had to keep sipping water to soothe my throat as I forced down bite after bite.

Josh took the plate when it was empty and set it on the little table next to my bed. "Shiro and Adam left right after you got back. We're hoping they'll be home soon with whatever Nirah needs."

I nodded. "Yeah, Mom said. Why didn't you go?"

He glanced at Mom. "No way she was letting me out of her sight. Not with you lying down here on the vent." He sighed. "You didn't look good there for a while."

I was pretty sure I didn't look good now. "Need to wash. Help me up."

Mom pulled the IV line out of my arm, holding off the puncture. We tried hard not to use the limited medical supplies we had left, and it drove home how bad off I must have been.

"Thanks, Mom."

She and Josh helped me up. My legs wobbled and my head still throbbed, but moving around was helping. I made it over to a basin and wiped down the worst of my stench with a clean rag.

"I want to sleep in my own bed," I said. Mom looked dubious, but Josh threw an arm under my shoulder. "I'll get you to your room. Malia's gonna be awfully glad to see you."

The walk through the cavernous hallways to my room felt as long as any of the journeys I had made in the forest or over the mountains, but when I got to my own bed it was worth it.

I collapsed into it and Josh fussed around, pulling up my blankets and filling up a mug of water to set by my bed.

"I'm fine," I mumbled. "Just tired."

He set the mug down. "I know. Takes more than a thorn bush to take down a Wilde." His face sobered for a moment. "Really thought we lost you this time, buddy. Sure glad to see you up and around."

"Tomorrow I'm going to head down to Eden Base and help Shiro and Nirah."

Josh laughed. "Yeah, we'll see. Maybe not tomorrow." He paused in the doorway, pulling up the hanging fabric that closed off my room. "We're going to get Dad back. No matter what. Now get some rest."

He ducked under the fabric and I sank into my blankets, and into dreamless sleep.

CHAPTER 20

SHIRO

I slept poorly, my head pillowed on my pack on the hard, tilted floor, and rain pelting against the thick windows. When the morning sun brightened the interior, I stretched and hopped to my feet.

The eggs had hatched overnight.

Mama Rex was nowhere to be seen, but three babies stirred in the log nest across the base. Their heads kept peeping up over the edges, peering around at everything. They made no sound, at least none that I could hear through the walls of the transport.

"Adam, check it out," I whispered. "The babies hatched."

He moved in beside me, scratching at his hair. "This thing is filthy. How did we live here for three years?" He pressed his face against the glass. "Great. More Rexes. Just what we needed."

Mama must have been out hunting, because when she returned, she stood next to the nest and sniffed at her babies. They hopped around, shoving each other out of the way to get near her huge head. With a great heave, she threw up a putrid pile of meat into the nest, which the babies descended on like a Wolf pack. They tore at the softened 'saur flesh, gobbling down chunks. When one of them tried to swallow a piece that was too big, it hacked until it brought the chunk back up. Its brother jumped on the piece and snapped it down.

"Nasty. Those things will eat anything." Adam turned away from the window and shoved Don with his foot to wake him up.

I sighed and considered our options. Too late to try and roll the eggs away from base. Too late to crush them and take our chances. The baby Rexes were almost as tall as I was when they stood up straight, and although I doubted they had any hunting skills, I wasn't about to go out and test them.

We decided to focus on the parts we could get from inside the transport. With luck, the Rex family would move out of the base by the time we were ready to get the parts we needed from the outside of the ship.

They didn't leave. After four days we had pulled apart the cockpit and engine control room, making piles of the equipment Nirah wanted to fix the shuttle. She and Don argued constantly.

"We haven't modified the thrusters at all. If we fix it back to standard spec, it will never get out into orbit. We can't get the power."

"I'm working on it," Nirah muttered. She spent a lot of time on her trans, and when I peeked over her shoulder, the calculations she was working on filled the whole screen. "If we took the transport engine, we'd get the power."

Don shook his head. "But the weight would offset it. Still wouldn't get out of the atmosphere."

She glared at him. "I know that." She looked back at her trans. "But if we could offset the weight . . . " Her fingers flew over the screen while Don looked on.

"There are twelve people on Horizon," he said, peering over her shoulder. "Even if the only person going up is a pilot, there will be thirteen people coming down. Plus weapons, medical equipment. All the things we left behind."

"I know that," Nirah repeated. She shot me a glance that I interpreted to mean, *If you don't get him out of my face, the Rex won't matter because I'm going to kill him myself.* Don had that effect on a lot of people.

"Hey, Don," I said. "Can you give me a hand over here?" There wasn't much for me to do until we could get outside, but I was sorting the parts we'd collected into piles. One of the other transports should still have a wheeled flatbed in it, which we planned to hitch to the back of the tank so we could haul all this junk back to Carthage. It would never fit inside. But first we had to get out to the other transport without becoming a meal for the baby Rexes just a stone's throw away.

Three more days passed and the Rexes didn't leave. We were too close, trapped in the transport, for tempers to stay calm much longer. Don was getting frantic, knowing his daughter was awaiting our shuttle on board Horizon. I was watching the days pass, each one bringing us closer to the Flood. And I was desperate to know that Caleb was all right. There was still no connection on the sat trans, which didn't help Don's panic one bit.

"All right," Adam said finally. "The adult is usually gone for an hour or two when she hunts. We can set an armed watch on top of the transport and leave the outside door open. From up there we should see her coming, or anything else, in time to get everyone back inside and the door shut before it gets here."

Nobody liked that plan. But nobody could think of anything better.

We took turns on sentry duty: me, Adam, and Fernando. Nirah and Don scuttled around the ship with whoever wasn't on watch, peering over their shoulders and not getting much accomplished. They found the flatbed and hauled it around, but the largest parts had to get loaded first, and those were still attached to the transports.

I had to admit that the babies were almost cute. I preferred sentry duty to following Nirah around with a blowtorch, pulling the engine apart. Part of the solar panel on top of the transport had shifted, making a nice protected spot for me to shelter from the sun, and to hide when pterosaurs cruised by overhead. I watched the babies, which seemed to get bigger every day.

The largest was a bully, and I called him Godzilla. *Caleb would love that.* I called the middle one Ani, which was the Japanese word for "brother." The smallest, Little Runt, was looking thin, and wasn't as fast as the others. It had to settle for the scraps left by its larger siblings, and I wondered how often a Rex was able to raise three babies without losing one. They were strong enough to climb out of the nest now, and the two larger ones, Godzilla and Ani, would roll around the middle of the clearing, snapping at each other and chasing around the nest. When Mama returned and barfed up their dinner, they rushed in and claimed the best parts. Little Runt cleaned up whatever was left, and Mama didn't seem to care that one of her babies was rapidly losing ground.

I never saw Mama's mate. I had no idea if this was normal, and the male usually abandoned his family, or if something had happened to him. Sometimes we heard the calls of a Rex in the distant jungle when Mama was out hunting, but no male ever appeared near the nest.

The day was heating up and I squatted in the shade of the solar panel, rifle at the ready. Movement in the trees caught my eye and I whistled the signal for everyone to get inside. They were working on one of the other ships and I could see them all scuttle in.

Mama Rex lumbered into the clearing. The babies clustered around her, making excited little noises. She leaned over and heaved up a pile of meat.

A flash of color caught my eye.

Ani pulled at a chunk of meat, and the bright blue was evident in the pile of dark, soft vomit.

I knew that color. I remembered it well. It was a shirt, and the last time I had seen it, it had been worn by Cari Cooper, one of the survivors of Transport Seventeen. I remembered exactly how it looked when she bolted into the jungle at the edge of a ravine, never to be seen again until this moment.

Cari had been terrified of heights. On the way back from where their ship had landed, we'd had to cross a deep gorge. Caleb climbed all the way down and back up the other side, which allowed us to stretch a rope across. I was the first one over and we tied another rope for everyone to use: one to stand on, shuffling their feet across, and the other to hold on to. Everyone made it over, and only Adam was left on the far side with Cari.

Caleb and I had watched her over the ravine. She wouldn't get near the edge. Adam grabbed her arm and tried to pull her toward the ropes, and she bolted away into the jungle. I had wanted to cross back over and try to find her, but Caleb said we had to go on without her. He was right. We couldn't risk the rest of the group to try and bring back one wayward member. And I doubted I'd have any better luck getting her out onto those ropes than Adam had. But it was devastating to walk away, knowing one of our own was left on the other side, defenseless in a jungle she had no idea how to survive in.

She'd obviously done well. Maybe she'd been dead for a while, and the Rex had just found her, but I doubted it. If something else had killed her, there wouldn't have been enough left for me to see the color of her shirt. Somehow she'd survived longer than I would have ever imagined out on her own. Until now.

"Fly free, Cari Cooper," I murmured as the baby Rex made the bright blue shirt disappear.

CHAPTER 21

CALEB

Word got out about the possibility of the Flood coming to our valley. Everybody in Carthage knew that my dad and the others were still alive up on Horizon, but we had tried to keep secret the possibility that a hoard of little hungry 'saurs might swarm us in just over a month. There was no point in panicking everybody when we were doing all we could.

We shouldn't have worried. Most of our people didn't believe it would happen here. We'd never seen a Flood at our old base, and they couldn't imagine we weren't safe here. But I'd seen so much more out in the jungle than they had. And I trusted Nirah. There was nothing more we could do until Shiro's team got back with the parts for the shuttle, but I chafed inside with nothing to do to prepare for what I believed was coming.

Staci was at my side every step I took. She hadn't forgiven me for leaving on the mission to retrieve Nirah's people without saying goodbye. But I was never big on goodbyes. There had been too many. Mom said she had spent every day next to my bed while I was unconscious, only leaving to eat. She hadn't forgiven me for waking up when she wasn't there, either, but she made sure I always had a plate of food, and a padded spot to sit in the sunshine on the plateau, soaking in the heat while we waited for word from Shiro.

My strength was coming back slower than I liked, and I leaned on Staci as we headed outside in the cool of the morning. Ryenne was already out at the little shed where her young 'saur pets slept, and as we approached, I could see that Carmen was helping her clean up their fenced yard.

"Caleb!" Ryenne dropped her rake and ran over to throw her arms around me. "Are you all right? Your mom said you were awake but I shouldn't come visit so you could rest."

I grinned at my cousin. "I'm okay. Not ready to take on a Rex quite yet, but I'm getting there."

Her eyes darted back to where her 'saurs were poking their noses out the shed door. "They're growing so fast. Sara says they'll start laying eggs pretty soon."

Carmen snorted. "That's the last thing I want to see here."

I turned to look at her. "What do you mean? We need more of these little guys all laying eggs as soon as we can. Eggs are really delicious."

She shook her head. "Not these kind, whatever they are. I know eggs are good. We used to dig them up back at our old camp."

"Dig them up?" I shared a glance with Staci. We didn't know of any 'saurs that buried their eggs.

"Yeah," she said. "The Flood beasts." She never called them 'saurs. Probably hadn't realized they were dinosaurs at all. "They would come through every year. When the females came back through a couple of weeks later, we killed all we could. But some of them didn't get through, anyway. Most of them headed off north to lay their eggs, where it's cooler I guess, but some of them stopped in our area. Maybe tired, I don't know. They'd dig a deep hole and crawl into it, and pull the dirt back on top of themselves. Nirah dug some up later and found out they were laying their eggs underground, then dying right on top of them. When the eggs hatched, the babies would eat the dead mother before digging themselves out. That's when they'd head south."

I gaped at her. Sara had never talked about any kind of 'saur doing that. She was going to flip when she heard this.

Carmen looked around the valley. "If they come through here, there will probably be some. Probably not many, 'cause most of them make it way farther north. That's where the millions of them hatch out. North somewhere. But I bet we could find some here if we looked."

All my weariness flowed away. "Do you know where they'd be?"

Sara will freak if we bring her Flood eggs. And everyone would stop doubting they were coming, and . . . I trailed off that thought. *And panic.* But we had to look.

Carmen set down the bucket she was carrying and pointed across the field. "They like that kind of pine tree. If they're here, that's where they'll be."

All four of us looked at each other for a moment.

"Hand me that shovel and let's go." I held out my hand and Ryenne snorted. "I'll carry it. You're not strong enough yet."

We left the 'saur pen, closing the gate behind us. Ryenne's babies chirped at the fence as we walked away.

"They sure do love you," Staci said. "It's cool that they think you're their mom."

Ryenne made a face. "I'm just glad they're not Flood 'saurs. Don't want them eating my dead body."

Past the orchard of fruit trees on the other side of the lake was a small copse of pine trees. They had long, soft needles and the air smelled crisp and fresh.

"Here. Let's look here," Carmen said. "Back where we were, they always buried themselves near this kind of tree. There are a lot more of them the farther north you go, apparently."

It took all morning to find the mound Carmen was looking for. I let the girls do most of the walking, content to sit in the cool shade among the fallen pine needles. At the sound of Carmen's yell, I jumped to my feet and jogged over to where she stood.

"Here." She pointed to a small mound of dirt mostly covered in dry pine. "Dig here."

I reached for the shovel, but Staci grabbed it faster. "You sit," she said with a frown at me. "I'll dig."

It only took her a few minutes of scraping at the dry soil.

"Oh, gross." She jumped back from the hole. "There's something squishy in there. It stinks."

It did stink. I grabbed the shovel and uncovered a small, putrefying mound of flesh. It was about the size of my head, soft and smelly. The skull was flat and full of teeth, and it appeared to have four legs, though the shovel had destroyed three of them.

Carmen stared into the hole.

"The eggs will be underneath the body."

They were.

Each one larger than my fist, they had soft, leathery shells. I used the shovel to move the remains of the mother aside and scooped one of the eggs up. The shovel's blade tore the soft shell easily, and a thick, yellow fluid oozed out, followed by a small, curled-up green lump.

It moved when I touched it.

"Leave it alone!" Carmen had backed up into the trees, and peered out through the branches. "It might be ready to hatch."

It wasn't. Even I could tell that. But when I uncurled the sticky little half-formed thing, it had the same flat, tooth-filled head as its dead mother.

There were at least thirty eggs in the hole. I took off my shirt and piled the eggs on it, making a little carrying pouch.

Sara's going to freak out. And so is everyone else.

The Flood had passed through this valley last year.

They were coming.

CHAPTER 22

SHIRO

The next morning Godzilla was gone. We hadn't heard anything in the night, and didn't bother keeping watch once we were all safely inside the transport. Godzilla had been venturing farther from the nest, while Ani and Little Runt stayed closer under the protective wing of the transport. I crouched on the roof of the ship, scanning the clearing, but the little bully was nowhere to be seen. When Mama Rex returned from her hunting trip, she smelled all around the clearing, nostrils flaring, before she herded the remaining two babies into the remnants of the nest. She kept watch all day and we all huddled inside the stifling transport waiting for her to leave.

Nirah was chafing, pacing around the dim interior.

Don, as ever, was needling her with questions. "Could we remove a couple of the control rods and get more thrust?"

I leaned back against the transport wall. They were always going on like that.

"If we remove the control rods, we risk overheating the fission reactor. They're called control rods for a reason."

Don grabbed her trans, scowling at the calculations. "It wouldn't explode. But it might give us enough power to leave atmosphere."

They argued in technical terms I didn't understand.

Adam emerged from the cockpit of the transport. "I got through to Carthage for a couple of minutes. Talked to the Mayor. Caleb is okay."

All the breath left me in a whoosh. *Caleb is okay. Thank the shining stars.*

"But Carmen found something in our valley," Adam continued. "The sat was breaking up, but it was something about eggs. I couldn't hear everything, but he just kept saying, 'It's coming. It's coming.'"

Nirah cursed. "I told them and nobody listened. Flood 'saurs bury their eggs. If they found them in the valley, then we're right in their path."

"Are we doing all this for nothing?" He pulled a piece of dried meat out of our shared stash, which was growing alarmingly small.

I shrugged. "They'll figure something out. No way we could get all the way to Tau Ceti from Earth but can't figure out how to make a rocket launch."

Nirah glared at me. "We're not launching a rocket. We're trying to get a shuttle high enough in the air. The higher it is, the less drag from air in the atmosphere. If we get the shuttle high enough, it will get easier to fly and should be able to make it into orbit. That's what they were designed to do."

She thought for a moment. "The old rockets on earth were launched straight up. They were basically a capsule sitting on a huge bomb that shot them right up into the sky."

"So let's make one," I said.

Don snorted. "We don't have anywhere near what we'd need to redesign a shuttle and build booster rockets."

The shuttle vibrated. Mama Rex was on the move.

"Maybe we don't have to." Nirah's face was lit by the trans in her hands. "If we could create a big enough explosion right under the shuttle, if it was already flying straight up . . ." She dove back into her calculations. After a few moments she grinned at Don. "I think we need to remove some control rods."

Adam and I looked at each other, obviously thinking the same thing. *She's nuts.*

Don said it first. "You're insane. Nobody would risk a launch like that. No way Borin will ever authorize it. Not just to rescue a dozen people, no matter who they are." His voice choked on the last bit.

"Don's right," I said. "We've done some risky things to rescue people before, but you're talking about a nuclear blast. Almost certain death for whoever is in that shuttle." I shook my head. "Nobody's going to fly that mission."

Nirah's foot tapped on the transport floor, scattering dust that sparkled in the sunlight that streamed through the window. "It's the best I've got for now." She glanced out the window toward the Rex nest. "If we ever get out there to salvage, we'll take everything we can. I'll try to figure out some other way once we get back with the parts. Maybe with a couple months' work . . ."

I followed her gaze out the window. Nirah would think of something. *If we ever get out of this stifling transport and past that Rex.*

Mama Rex didn't leave her babies the next day, but the following morning she pounded out of the clearing. We scattered out of the transport, me climbing the ladder in the cargo bay to pop out the hatch on top and take my customary position under the solar panel's shade.

The two remaining babies, Ani and Little Runt, were rolling around in the middle of the circle, obviously relieved to be out from under Mama's watchful eye. She hadn't let them leave the nest for an entire day and night, and they were full of energy, and clumsy as they grew so fast. I grinned as I watched them at play. Soon they'd be fearful monsters, but today they looked like every movie I'd ever seen of puppies playing on someone's living room floor.

I never heard it coming.

Across the far side of the clearing, a huge iridescent black shape slithered into view.

Titanoboa.

I gave the whistle for the team to get inside, but couldn't take my eyes off the enormous snake creeping between the transports.

Right toward the babies. They huddled inside the nest, shaking with terror.

It was stupid, I know. The stupidest thing I could have done. If I'd stopped for two seconds to think, I would have hopped inside the transport and let the scatting snake eat those babies.

But I didn't. I raised my rifle and shot it right in the face.

The bullets bounced off, of course, and the snake paused in its approach, tongue flicking in and out, tasting the air. In a moment, it resumed its slither, heading for the baby Rexes.

I shot it six more times.

Shiro, you are an idiot. What on Ceti are you doing?

The snake reared up and hissed at me, black eyes boring into mine.

If Caleb were here, he'd never do anything this stupid.

I didn't even notice the shaking of the earth, and neither did the Boa. From between the transports, Mama Rex burst into the clearing, snapping her huge jaws around the snake's tail and shaking it like a dog. It flew out of her grasp and bounced off my transport, rocking the side. I dropped to my belly, hanging on to the solar panel's mooring as the ship swayed under me.

The Boa darted straight at Mama Rex. She stood in front of the nest, blocking her babies from the Boa's attack, and roared her challenge. The sound made my stomach drop right out of my body.

Idiot. Stupid, stupid, stupid.

The Boa feinted to the right and Mama missed her lunge. She snapped again at the huge predator, which latched its huge jaws onto her neck, coiling the top of its body around her upper torso. She strained and grabbed for its tail, but the Boa whipped itself out of range of her teeth, wrapping coil after coil around her. The ground shook as she fell, feet tangled in the writhing black serpent.

I knew how this ended.

Mama Rex struggled, and behind her the babies cried pathetic little bleats. The mother Rex was far too big for the Boa to eat, but I had no doubt that as soon as she was dispatched, Little Runt and Ani would join poor Godzilla in the Boa's stomach.

I'm a good shot. Always have been. Probably the best shot in Carthage. But the shot I made that morning . . . the stupid, stupid shot I made . . .

I jumped to my feet and raised my rifle. *You're an idiot. If Caleb were here . . .*

But Caleb wasn't there. There was only me, Shiro Yamoto, and I made the shot.

The Boa's left eye exploded as my bullet hit it straight on.

It shuddered and let go of its hold on Mama's neck.

She reached one giant hind foot up and clawed straight into the snake's belly, kicking it free as it flung itself around. Her jaws snapped onto its head and crunched.

The Boa shuddered and fell from her shoulders. Mama Rex leaped clear of it and whacked it with her tail, sending it flying straight towards me.

I hit the deck, grabbing for purchase as the transport rocked under me again. The Boa was so close I could smell it, and I peeked over the edge of the transport. It laid there, blood on its shining black scales.

Across the clearing, Mama Rex roared her triumph. The Boa turned and slithered away between the transports, disappearing into the river that flowed next to our abandoned base. I watched it submerge, the last of its tail sinking into the dark water.

"Fly free, Godzilla."

When I turned back to the clearing, Mama Rex was standing right next to my transport. Blood clotted in the teeth marks left on her neck, and she stared into my eyes.

Oh, scat.

She didn't move, and for an eternal moment, we regarded each other across the exceptionally small space between us. Her head was as tall as the transport, and I remembered the very first time I had seen a Rex, from this exact vantage point, in the early days before the electric wire.

Once again, there was no electric wire.

She sniffed once, nostrils flaring. I didn't breathe, eyes locked on hers.

She blinked once, turned around, and crept over to her crying babies.

I scuttled into the open hatch, squeaking it closed behind me.

All afternoon I watched her, ignoring the rebukes of my teammates. Yes, she knew we were here now. Yes, she probably always had. No, we were probably never getting out of here alive.

Mama Rex tended to her babies, occasionally glancing at our transport. She stayed until the sun dropped below the horizon and plunged the camp into the moonless dark.

And the next morning, Mama Rex and her babies were gone.

CHAPTER 23

CAPTAIN'S PERSONAL JOURNAL. YEAR 3, DAY 125

The reactor has failed.

We're going to have to make a decision soon. Horizon Alpha was supposed to remain in orbit for hundreds of years. When the reactors quit working, as we always knew they eventually would, the solar arrays were supposed to be enough to keep the ship powered, its thrusters keeping Ceti's gravity from pulling it down to crash on the surface. If a thruster became inoperable, the people on the planet were supposed to be able to initiate a controlled descent with a planned separation of each cylinder, ensuring that the parts of the ship crashed safely in an ocean on the other side of the world from where their colonies would have been.

None of that is happening. We lost a third of our solar arrays in the original disaster, and those that remain will not be enough to keep us in orbit for long. Our life support is powered, but our calculations indicate that within a year, we'll lose enough altitude to enter Ceti's atmosphere and crash. Some of the ship will burn up upon entry, but it's huge. Even if we can manage to get the cylinders to separate as programmed on the way down, we will have no control over where we finally crash. Of course there is no expectation that any of us could survive. We have escape pods designed to survive re-entry, with parachutes and their own thrusters to allow them to land, but after all this time and damage, they are unlikely to work. None of us are panicked about our impending deaths. But we are panicked for those on the planet below us.

We can't control where the ship will crash. And an impact of this size on the same continent as our people could create an extinction level event that will make the meteor strike that ended Earth's dinosaurs' time look like a dust storm. It's also a nuclear ship, so if the impact crater doesn't kill them all, the radiation might.

I'm trying to find a solution. Later this week I'll be doing a spacewalk to see if I can repair enough of the solar array to allow us to initiate the crash sequence and ensure that we crash on the opposite side of the planet from Eden Base.

It might be a moot point. They're almost out of power themselves. Caleb is going out tomorrow on a mission to get a power core from one of the wrecks they know about. Carthage is leading it, so I'm sure they'll be safe. But if they don't find it, Horizon Alpha can crash wherever she wants because no one but the dinosaurs will still be alive down there.

YEAR 3, DAY 214

They've found a place to live. We were full of joy as we heard their chatter, loading up their shuttles to evacuate to the valley Caleb and Josh found. I can't express my relief knowing that Randa and my daughter will finally have a safe place to live. And with a new baby on the way, that valley will be a fresh start for my family. My old friend Carthage fathered that baby, and I'm forever grateful to him for keeping Malia and Randa alive. He's gone now, but when Randa has the baby, a bit of him will live again. And my sons are finally safe as well, so in a way, a bit of me will live, too.

YEAR 3, DAY 276

We've been putting off the decision, but in another few months, we'll be out of options. We'll have to initiate the crash sequence to be sure that our loved ones on the planet below are safe. But they've found Transport Seventeen. My niece and nephew are on that transport, along with Bethany's father, Don, and Caleb is flying out to get them. For Bethany's sake, we can't go down before she knows that her father has made it back to Carthage Valley.

YEAR 3, DAY 299

They made it back. Most of them. I'm so incredibly proud of my son Caleb.

YEAR 3, DAY 301

They heard us. They know we're alive.

CHAPTER 24

CALEB

Shiro's team was gone for three more days.

Without the sat trans contact, we had no idea what was going on with the away team. We got a few minutes of signal here and there, enough to see that their sat trans were active, and moving around the base, so we knew they were alive, but the small amount of communication was spotty and usually cut off mid-sentence. They said something about a Rex, and something about an engine, but we couldn't make any sense of it.

Sara had, as expected, freaked out. She and Mayor Borin argued about showing the Flood 'saurs to everyone. Mayor Borin didn't want to confirm the rumor and risk panic. But Sara insisted we needed every able-bodied person out in the pine trees, digging up all the mounds we could find.

Sara was right.

We found another nine mounds over the next three days, and destroyed them. Nobody was certain we had gotten them all, but we continued stomping over every meter of ground in our valley, looking for the telltale signs.

Late in the afternoon, Erik rushed into the Painted Hall shouting, "They're back!" We had a guard stationed in the re-opened front door around the clock now, though we were so low on ammunition that if something really wanted to get in, there probably wasn't much a guard was going to do, other than let us know we were all about to get eaten.

Now I bolted down the narrow passageway, emerging into the bright sun. The tank was rumbling up far below me, emerging from the thick tree line. A wide trailer bounced along behind it, full of metal bits all lashed together into a jumble. They pulled in right next to the derelict shuttle and turned off the engine. The hatch popped and Shiro's head peeked through.

He disappeared, and Nirah climbed out, followed by Don, Fernando, and Adam. I expected them all to head for the crumbling path up toward the entrance to our cave system, but instead they immediately began tugging on the straps, releasing metal parts that clattered to the ground.

I peered around at the jungle edge, far too close to where they were working. Anything could be hiding in there, waiting for a chance to leap out and have a human-size snack. I waved down to the group, and Shiro squinted up at me. He dropped the thick black hose he was carrying and scrambled up the path.

"Caleb! Hey, you look awful!"

I gave him a hand up the final climb and he threw his arms around me, clapping me on the back and making me cough. "Easy, man. I was almost dead for a week."

Shiro stood back and peered at me up and down in the filtered light of the tunnel. "I didn't want to go. Didn't want to leave you like that." He glanced down at the little group unloading the trailer. "But we couldn't wait. And we didn't even know . . ." He trailed off.

"Didn't know if I was going to make it." I chuckled. "Yeah, Josh said the same thing. But I'm hard to kill."

He nodded, and smiled suddenly as something popped into his head. "You should have been there. Baby Rexes. Man, you should have seen it."

Nirah's team was still pulling things off the trailer. "You need to get them in here. Whatever she wants to do, we need to do it at night. Not safe out there in the daytime."

Shiro rolled his eyes. "Yeah, we sure know that. But getting Nirah to stop when she's on a roll . . ."

"She'll stop real fast if a Wolf pack hears all that racket." I grabbed one of the pitons embedded as a handhold in the rock, preparing to head down and try to make them come up for the afternoon, but Shiro headed me off.

"I'll get them in. You stay here."

He swung over the edge and down the narrow path. From below I could make out snippets of argument. Fernando kept looking out into the trees, and Don was hanging close to the tank as Nirah bustled around.

A distant roar cut through the air and the forest went silent.

The clatter of metal on dirt followed as the team scrambled for the path up to safety.

CHAPTER 25

CALEB

I sat on the plateau overlooking the valley, balancing my dinner plate on my lap. We had found three more Flood 'saur nests in the pine grove and Sara got more agitated with every egg we brought her. She was trying to come up with some kind of repellant, some chemical that might make them avoid our valley, but didn't seem to be making much progress.

Malia plopped down next to me and grabbed a handful of berries off my plate. "Mom said you need to rest," she said. "You need to come inside." She snuggled into my armpit, playing with the little doll Mom had made her. It was a birdman made out of twigs and wool, with crocheted feathers and a carved wooden beak.

"It's such a nice night, though." We shared my dinner under the bright, round moon.

Sara appeared next to us, holding her own plate. "Room for one more?"

Malia jumped up and hugged Sara's legs.

"Here, let me take that." I reached up to take Sara's plate so she could sit next to us on the smooth rocks, our feet dangling over the edge. "How's the work coming?" I didn't want to push her, but if Nirah's calculation was correct, the Flood would be here in a month or so. We still had no plan to survive them.

She picked at the food on her plate. "Nothing yet. We just don't have the facility to manufacture anything in the kind of quantity we'd need to go around the whole valley."

The full moon made everything in the valley look gray. If Sara came up with something that repelled the 'saurs, we'd need an awful lot of it.

"Careful, Mali." I grabbed the back of her shirt as she stood too close to the edge of the plateau, playing with her doll. She swooped it all around in her hands, flying it around as the real Birdmen almost certainly never did.

"What did they do?" Sara's voice was distant, contemplative.

"What did who do?"

"The Birdmen," she said. "The Flood isn't new. A migration like that doesn't just change course since they were here." She tapped her fingernail against the metal plate, looking up at the bright moon.

Her eyes snapped wide. "I need to see . . ." She cut off and turned to me. "Go get Ryenne. And a bunch of lanterns." She dropped the plate and jumped to her feet. "They did come here. And the Birdmen survived."

Sara, Ryenne, and I stood in one of the lowest reaches of our caverns. It was another painted room full of Birdmen drawings and their scratchy writing. Sara held the lantern up, muttering to herself as she circled the room. We had uncovered it in our continued exploration of some of the less accessible areas. The walls were smooth and regular, a clear sign of Birdman excavation.

"Here." She stopped and pointed at a peculiar series of drawings. "I knew I'd seen them. I just didn't know what they meant."

The pictures showed the form of a Birdman standing on a hill. There was a circle over his head and his mouth was open. Little lines were coming out of the beak. All around him the mountain was covered in little dots.

"I thought he was singing to the full moon," Sara said, and Ryenne nodded.

"It looks like he's singing."

Sara whirled to face her. "You said your little 'saurs run and hide when you practice your flute?"

Ryenne nodded. "They hate it. I keep telling them I'll get better with practice."

The lantern shone on the writing and Sara murmured as her eyes ran across the lines. "I didn't know so many of these words. I still don't." She turned to me, gesturing with the lantern. "But don't you think this looks like a million little 'saurs?"

The dots all over the mountains. Tiny, hungry 'saurs.

"Nirah said it's the first full moon after the equinox." I looked at the drawing. "That sure looks like a full moon."

"I was right about the words I knew, though," Sara said. "They are singing. Look here." The next picture showed a bunch of jagged lines. "See? It's a map of our valley. And all these circles and lines around the perimeter? I think that's where the Bird People stood. Where they stood and sang."

The next picture showed three suns and three moons. And the next showed the mountain without the dots.

"The 'saurs hate the noise." Ryenne's eyes lit up. "They were protecting their people."

Sara nodded, pointing to the suns. "I think you're right. The Bird People stood on the edges of the mountains that ring the valley and they sang for three days and three nights. To keep the Flood from coming into the valley."

I stared at Sara. "Three days straight?"

She shrugged. "I'm sure they took turns. But that has to be what this means."

There was no way we could close up the cave entrance to keep them out. These caves had a million tiny openings, and the main mouth into the valley was tall and wide. Even if we piled stone into it, they'd squeeze through. After they ate our sheep and probably all our crops.

"So we have to sing, too," Ryenne said. "How many flutes do we have? My 'saurs hate it." She pointed at the picture. "The Flood 'saurs must hate it, too. So we have to get enough people making enough noise to keep them out."

Sara shook her head. "There's no way. There aren't enough of us to make enough racket even if we had a flute for every person. We need something loud. All around the valley."

"Something like the speaker system on Horizon Alpha," I said.

They stared at me.

"Well, it would work, wouldn't it?" I looked at the picture of the Birdman shrieking for his life, keeping the Flood out of the valley. "If we pulled the whole system out of Horizon with all the wire and ran it all the way around? Blasted the warning siren?"

I remembered the siren well from the evacuation. Horizon had been on fire and the siren had screamed from every corner of the ship.

"It might." Sara picked up her lantern. "We would need . . . maybe fifty of the wall speakers. Enough wire to hook them all up, all the way around the valley. We can run the noise from a trans, so we don't need the Horizon computer. Just the speakers and the wires."

"What about my 'saurs?" Ryenne asked.

I looked around the cavern. "We can bring them way down here. Use a bunch of cloth to pad up the walls, soundproof it as best we can. They may not like it, but they'll survive."

My mind was spinning as we trooped back up the smooth stone staircase. We had lost Kintan retrieving Nirah. She was our only hope to get us flying again. But she could do it. If anyone could figure out a way to get a shuttle up to Horizon, Nirah could.

We had thought it was another rescue mission. My dad and the others were counting on us to save them from a half-dead, burned-out hulk in orbit. It was so much more than that now.

If we didn't get that sound system from Horizon, we'd have to abandon the caves and try to get back to the old Eden base transports while the Flood passed through. Mayor Borin in his wheelchair would never make it. The babies and the toddlers had no chance. We could lose half our people over a week in the jungle. If a Wolf pack found us, or a Rex . . . My mind turned away from the horror. We could lose everyone.

"Nirah has to get that shuttle flying, and fast." I followed Sara up the stairs. "We've got four weeks to get ready for the Flood."

CHAPTER 26

CAPTAIN'S PERSONAL JOURNAL. YEAR 3, DAY 322

Nirah Saffar thinks she can get a shuttle to us. Her idea is completely insane, but that's classic Nirah. I'm torn in half by their plan. The shuttle crew is just as likely to be killed in the attempt to get up here as they are to make it to Horizon. If it were only about us, I would forbid them from attempting it. But it's not just about us. They need the speakers from Horizon, the wired system throughout the ship that carried our emergency alerts and ship wide announcements. The alert system is destroyed, but we'll be able to salvage a lot of the speakers. And if Sara Arnson is right, the noise they make might spare the valley from the millions of tiny dinosaur predators that almost wiped out Nirah's entire group. So this insane mission is not just about rescuing us.

But it is also about rescuing us.

I had given up hope so long ago. And after all the mistakes I've made, the idea that I could live out the rest of my days on an actual planet fills me with a hope that shames me. So many others deserved to live before me.

We begin today dismantling the speakers and collecting the equipment. If the shuttle makes it to us, it will dock at the fore side of the central axis, so that's where we'll put it all, attaching it to the wall nets so it doesn't float away. If they make it, we'll have an easy time loading it all up in zero gravity.

If they make it.

CHAPTER 27

CALEB

Every night things got more tense as the clock ticked down to the Flood's arrival. We watched the stars twinkling over our dark valley, waiting for the appearance of Tau Ceti d which rose just before the equinox and would herald our doom. Nirah and her team worked frantically on the shuttle through the nights, while Don took apart one of the transport's reactors, hiding his body behind an old metal door to protect him against the radiation. There was nothing he could do about his hands and arms, but if he couldn't turn the reactor into an explosive, it wouldn't matter how much radiation he was exposed to because we'd all be dead when the Flood arrived.

The plan was insane. Nirah had explained it to the council as soon as her party returned from the old Eden Base. Step one was to get the shuttle flying again, using the parts they had scavenged from the transports we left behind. But there was no way to boost the shuttle's thrusters enough to get it into the stratosphere. Every way she worked the numbers, the power came up short. Bolting on one of the huge transport's thrusters would make it too heavy to take off at all.

So we were going to set off a nuclear bomb.

Just a small one.

We had pored over the maps of the planet, looking for the perfect place to blow up Don's repurposed reactor. It needed to be far enough from Carthage not to endanger our people, but close enough that we could get there within a week or two in the tank. We were looking for something like a volcano, where the explosion would be directed mostly up, not out. If we could time it just as the shuttle was beginning its climb overhead, Nirah thought the detonation could lift the shuttle high enough for its thrusters to make it the rest of the way out of Ceti's pull.

I thought she was completely insane.

Far to the southeast, the green of the forest gave way to brown desert. Dozens of round pits were likely caldera, left when ancient volcanoes erupted in Ceti's distant past. We couldn't tell how deep they were, but they were our best chance.

Of course I was going.

And of course Mom freaked out.

I was sitting in the infirmary getting checked out for the hundredth time since I woke up. Standing up too fast still made me dizzy, but my strength was coming back. By the time the bomb was ready, I was certain I'd be in shape to lead the detonation party.

"Please, Caleb," Mom said, looking at the heart monitor stuck to my chest. "You don't always have to be the one to go. You're not ready. Let someone else take this one."

The beeping monitor echoed in the little cave room.

"I have to go, Mom. You know that. It's Dad up there. How can I not go?" I scratched at the pads stuck to my skin. "Shiro is going with me. He'll keep us safe."

She shook her head. "Nobody can keep anybody safe forever."

I shrugged. "Of course not. But this will be easy for the ground team. Out, set off the bomb, come back. We've got Don in case something goes wrong with the detonation, and me and

Shiro have the most experience in the jungle."

"You're not going to the jungle. Nobody has any experience in the desert."

The thought made my heart speed up, beeping away on the monitor. "Nope. We'll be the first to see it."

Mom sighed. "I know I can't forbid you to go. But you have to know how hard this is for me. Watching you leave again." She pulled the leads off my chest and I shimmied back into my shirt.

"I know. And I'll be careful. But this is for Dad. We're going to get him back."

Her eyes got a faraway look, the way they always did now that we knew he was still alive up there. "Careful. I don't even know what that means anymore."

There was never really any doubt that I was going to be part of the detonation team.

Mayor Borin had already alerted the Horizon survivors to our plight. In halting Morse Code, they had signaled that they would start pulling out the speakers and gathering all the wire they could pull so it was ready when we got there.

When we got there. *Horizon Alpha, home of the eternal optimists.*

We weren't sure who was going to be flying in the shuttle along with Nirah and Raphael, the pilot, but there were no volunteers. Apparently no one thought flying in a shuttle while a nuclear bomb was exploded underneath it was a good idea. Nirah said she was fine to be a crew of one, since if they reached Horizon they'd be adding eleven more people for the return trip, and if they didn't . . . Well, the fewer lost, the better. But we worried that docking the shuttle onto Horizon might require a spacewalk, since we were having spotty communication with the ship and weren't sure we'd be able to let them know when the shuttle was coming. They were supposed to operate a robotic arm that would grab hold of the shuttle and pull it into the docking station, but if no one was there to run it, someone would have to leave the shuttle and manually attach the arm to its port, then scoot across to the hatch on Horizon and open it from the outside. Hard to believe people weren't lining up for that job.

It might have been a different story if Erik hadn't died.

Since the months they spent alone in a cave just under our tunnel system, Erik and my brother Josh had been best friends. Erik never fully recovered from the bullet wound to his leg, and walked with a pronounced limp. Occasionally the leg would crumble underneath him and he'd fall, dismissing it with a laugh and a joke.

This time it gave way at the top of the long stone staircase that led outside.

It was the middle of the night and no one was on the stairs to catch him. He must have let go of the railing.

We found him at the bottom of the stairs with his neck broken. Mom said he would have died instantly.

Grief makes people do strange things. And the loss of his friend apparently made Josh go crazy, because he volunteered for the shuttle flight to go rescue our Dad.

CHAPTER 28

CALEB

The tank's interior smelled like dirty feet. We had room to move since the party was only Shiro, me, Don, and Adam, but the ventilation system had failed long ago and it was hot and damp inside. We took turns driving, popping out only to stretch our legs and water the trees. We had sat trans signal again, though it was unreliable, and we stayed relatively on course, plowing through the forest day and night. Through the thick windows I watched the jungle roll by, herds of startled 'saurs lumbering away from our noisy approach. We never turned the engine off, for fear it might not start again. Don was nowhere near the engineer that Nirah was, and he might not be able to fix it if it failed.

On the fifth day, the trees grew shorter and farther apart. Soon they were replaced in my window by scrubby bushes like the ones that grew among the rocky hills around our valley. The herds of grazers and browsers disappeared and the ground became flat and hard. We had arrived in the desert.

The heat was unbearable in the tank. We popped the top

for ventilation, pulling the dry air into our lungs. Sand blew in the top and Don made us close it, worrying that the grit might get into the instruments. The trailer we dragged behind us was covered in canvas, hiding the makeshift bomb we were towing.

Don had assured us it wasn't dangerous.

"The detonator is separate," he had said as we loaded the tank with food and water for the trip. "We won't put it together until we get there, and it can't blow on its own."

I wasn't convinced, but so far we hadn't exploded.

Shiro and I had speculated about what kind of 'saurs might live in the desert, but so far it seemed like there was nothing big enough to worry about. When we paused to water the desert, there was nothing but sand and dry rock. I made the mistake of lifting one of the rocks, and discovered a nest of brown, flat bugs bigger than my foot. They waved nasty-looking pincers at me and I dropped the rock, jumping back.

"Careful." Shiro shoved me away. "We don't know what's poisonous out here."

"Probably everything," I said.

Nights were surprisingly chilly, with a brisk wind that blew sandy grit into every orifice. When I chewed on the dried meat strips we had brought, I could feel the grit crunching between my teeth. I wrapped a strip of cloth around my face and spent hours riding on top of the tank, watching the empty brown sand blowing into little tornadoes all around me.

Six days into the journey, we saw the first rise.

It was a good satellite day and we pinpointed our location: exactly on target. The first of the round calderas was straight ahead.

Once we found the right pit, we would take a day to set up. The shuttle crew would fly out on the seventh morning, intending to rendezvous with us here that afternoon. We had enough charged power cores to run the shuttle and the tank, but we would use the solar receivers to top up the power in the shuttle before attempting the launch the following evening. If everything went well, the shuttle crew could get to Horizon, load up the equipment and survivors, and return to land at Carthage with a week to spare before the Flood. As soon as we got them headed skyward, we'd turn the tank around for the long journey back, arriving a day or so before we expected the millions of voracious little beasts to descend on our valley. By then, the people of Carthage should have had the equipment set up and ready to blast out the noise that should turn the Flood away from us.

Plenty of time. *Assuming every single insane thing we're attempting goes perfectly the first time we attempt it.*

We parked at the bottom of the first caldera, a steep, rugged hillside that climbed up out of the sand. Shiro and I jumped out of the tank, followed by Adam.

"Don's staying inside." Adam closed the hatch behind him. "Getting the detonator ready."

I grinned. "That's all he's done since we left. Pretty sure it's ready by now." Don would never have come out here if his daughter wasn't one of those stranded on Horizon. I remembered her from my childhood. She was about five years older than me, a fun-loving girl who was training to be an engineer like her dad. *It'll be good to see her again.* Nothing else would have ever gotten Don beyond Carthage's hills again. At least we didn't have to cross any water.

The thought made me lick my dry lips and reach for my canteen. I took a sip and followed Shiro up the hill, scanning all around us. Nothing moved in the late afternoon heat. Nothing out here was as dumb as we were, climbing through the arid furnace.

We were looking for some very specific parameters. The caldera we wanted had to be deep enough to contain the force of the blast upward, and wide enough not to blow apart from that force. We had hoped we might find one that was deep on the inside but not too steep on the outside so we could just drive the tank right up to the edge, but so far nothing we had seen indicated we would get that lucky. The bomb weighed a couple hundred kilograms—far too heavy for us to drag into position ourselves. The winch and cable on the front of the tank would have to do the work.

Shiro and Adam stopped at the top of the ridge and I clambered up behind them, trying not to pant with the effort. I wasn't back to full strength yet, though I never would have admitted that to Mom.

"This one's no good. Way too wide." Shiro pointed across the deep pit.

From this height, we could see a few other ridges in the distance. Adam peered through our binoculars and I crouched down, pretending to pull a rock out of my boot but actually catching my breath. Shiro raised an eyebrow at me.

Never could fool him.

"That one." Adam indicated a ridge just south of our location. "Looks promising."

Down we went, skidding on the steep surface. At the bottom, Adam climbed back down into the tank, and Shiro and I sat on top as we rumbled over to the next likely spot. Shiro was rubbing his leg where I knew it still pained him to climb like this.

It was perfect. Just high enough to contain the explosion, and narrow enough to force it upwards. The walls were thick at the bottom and wouldn't blow out when the bomb went off. We would be safely away by then, detonating it via a sat trans that Don had rigged. All we had to do was send the message, and the electricity from the device's charge would melt the wires we would place around the bomb, setting off chemical explosions that would detonate the nuke inside.

There was a wide, tall stone at the top that we could use as a pulley, wrapping the tank's cable around it to winch up the trailer containing the bomb. Then we would tip it over the edge and slowly lower it down to the bottom of the caldera. We would finish the wiring of the detonator at the bottom of the pit, climb out with the winch to help us, and meet the shuttle for the next day's launch.

Simple. Easy. Totally insane.

★★★

We spent the evening preparing to place the bomb. The winch would drag the whole trailer up the steep side and lower it back down the interior, so it had to be securely fastened from all sides. The entire thing was encased in a metal cube about waist high. There were a bunch of sharp edges where it had been removed from the transport it had powered, and some of those had sawed through the ropes that bound it onto the trailer. I was still uneasy touching the thing, but Don assured us it was totally safe.

"See here?" He pointed to a couple of indentations in the cube. "That's where we'll wire up the detonator. Can't blow until we tell it to."

No 'saurs had been sighted since we left the jungle, so Don was acting much braver, strutting around and telling us what to do. I kept reminding myself that he had as much stake in this rescue as I did. So many of us had loved ones on Horizon.

Shiro dragged the heavy metal cable up the side and looped it around the rock protrusion. When he returned with the rest of the cable, I helped him hook it to the trailer.

"All clear!" I called, and Adam engaged the winch.

The cable wound around the bar on the front of the tank with a whine of the engine. It slowly grew taut and I held my breath, willing it not to snap. The engine squealed, and with a lurch, the trailer moved.

"Steady it all the way up," Don said. He was standing behind the trailer and Shiro waved for him to move, muttering to me.

"Idiot doesn't have the sense not to stand underneath a bomb."

I grinned at him. "He has the sense not to be the ones to climb up a hill and tip a bomb over the edge."

Shiro's scowl made me laugh.

We climbed slowly as the winch dragged the trailer higher and higher on the hillside. The satellite coverage here was good, and just before we reached the top, I called to Adam on the trans.

"Almost there. Slow it down. Little by little until we get it around."

This was the most dangerous part. The cable was attached

to the front of the trailer, and it would have to swing around the rock pulley for us to get it onto the other side. There wasn't much flat surface at the top of the ridge, and if we lost control, the whole thing could crash down either side. Don promised us it wouldn't explode even if that happened, but if it was damaged, it wouldn't matter that we weren't killed by a nuclear blast. We'd be dead in about ten days when the Flood came anyway.

The trailer inched forward, and Shiro and I stood on the downside, shoving it sideways with all our strength. Our boots slid on the rocks as the trailer's edge caught on the rock we had wrapped the pulley around.

"Gotta get it all the way over," Shiro panted. "Push!"

We pushed. The cable ground against the rock, and the metal of the trailer groaned against the pressure. The back of the trailer skidded up over the side and the whole thing balanced on the edge for a few seconds before the cable pulled it further around.

I lunged for the edge of the trailer as it tipped over the inside of the ridge, and Shiro grabbed my arm, holding me back.

"Let it go!" He yelled into my sat trans, "Adam, stop!"

The grinding ended and the trailer hung over the edge, its back wheels in the air. We peered over the side. The inner edge was almost straight down for a couple of meters before it became a steep slope down to the bottom.

"Okay. Let's do this."

Shiro and I looked at each other and both took a deep breath. One on each side, we grabbed the cable and put a foot on the front of the trailer.

I spoke into my trans. "Okay, Adam. Let us down slow."

The engine sound whined from down the hill and the trailer, with us hanging onto it, backed off the edge. The whole thing went vertical for a few terrifying moments before the back wheels struck the inner edge. We rode the trailer down into the caldera inch by inch.

Please don't break. Please don't break. I implored the cable to hold us. If it let go, we would roll all the way down to the bottom. And even if we survived that, we'd never be able to climb out without the cable's support. It was too steep even for me at full strength, which I wasn't.

After what felt like an hour of descending, the ground started to level out beneath us. We hopped off the trailer and guided it the last few meters into the middle of the bowl-shaped depression.

"Okay, Adam, stop right there!" The cable stopped and we heaved a huge sigh. "We're here. Come on down."

Watching Don and Adam climb over the top of the ridge and down the cable was almost as harrowing as hanging on the trailer when we went over. Adam was a strong climber and carried the detonator in a pack on his back. Don was a clumsy mess.

"If he falls . . ." Shiro didn't have to finish. If Don fell, we were done. None of us knew how to set up the charge to blow this bomb.

I watched him come down.

Hang on. No, don't put your foot there. Keep your boots on the wall. I directed him silently. Adam was on the cable below him and we could hear him calling instruction up the line, the same things I was saying in my mind.

Finally they made it down. Don collapsed, gasping for air. Shiro sighed and handed him a canteen, which he drained in one long drink.

We let him rest for a few minutes before Adam opened the pack.

"All right. Let's get this ready to blow."

The edge of the caldera was throwing deep shadows by the time we had it rigged to Don's satisfaction. The sat trans that would get the signal to detonate was attached and left in standby mode. A sequence of five numbers was required to initiate the detonation just to make sure nobody set it off by accident. Don and Nirah had figured that from the time the signal was sent, it would take about two minutes for the wires to heat to melting temperature, setting off the mini-explosions that would trigger the bomb. The shuttle would be sweeping right up the side to be in position straight over the blast, and the force would shoot it skyward.

It was full dark when we got Don up the edge, with Adam in front and Shiro behind him. I climbed up last, gazing back over my shoulder at the bomb sitting silent at the bottom of the hole. My brother was going to be straight overhead when that bomb exploded.

I shivered in the chilly desert wind and started down the outside to wait out the night in the tank.

CHAPTER 29

JOSH

If there was anything worse than watching my little brother take off into the jungle in that tank, I don't know what it could have been.

I had stood at the tunnel entrance long after the rumble faded into the distance, breathing in the cool morning air that smelled so fresh up here.

The bright sun cast long shadows off the mountain, and I stayed in the cool of the cave entrance like a child waiting for his dad to come home.

He'd watched me take off in a tank just like that one, several long months ago. He'd found me out here where I'd come to hide from the world. Just me and Erik, and my shame and failure. Caleb had brought me out of the deep depression that had claimed me when I blamed myself for the deaths of my whole squad. He showed me it wasn't really my fault. And together, he and I brought the world back to these caves, where I started to feel alive again.

Until Erik fell.

The darkness that almost ended me months ago had returned, hungrier than ever. Erik was dead. Caleb was gone. And Dad was alive, waiting for a rescue that was almost certainly doomed to failure.

I came out again the evening before we were scheduled to take off and fly down to where Caleb and his team were setting up our launch site. Nirah was supervising the final repairs to the shuttle on the forest floor below my perch. I sat in the mouth of the tunnel as the last of the light faded from the sky, and they turned on their work lamps. It was risky, but necessary. Night was safer than daytime. Didn't I know it.

"When is Caleb coming home?" My little sister Malia had crept up behind me and plopped down on the ledge next to me.

"Another week, sweetie," I said. She leaned against me and I wrapped an arm around her shoulder.

"When are you coming home?"

She didn't understand any of this. I envied her that. She didn't know about the Flood, or about her father, stranded in space since she was a baby. She didn't remember Dad at all. But she knew I was leaving in the morning, and she remembered the last time I left her.

I couldn't lie to her again.

"I don't know, sweetie. I hope soon."

She snuggled in tighter under my arm. "Are you flying away? Up to the stars?"

"Yes." I peered into the dark sky, looking for the bright speck of Horizon Alpha. It was there, just below the crooked belt of Orion. I pointed at it. "That's the star I'm going to."

She looked up at the sky. "As long as the stars shine . . ."

I finished the sentence. "That's how long I'll love you." Our dad used to say that to us when we were little kids. Mom said it to Malia every night.

She didn't protest when I pulled her into my lap and buried my face in her soft, pale hair. *That's how long I'll love you.*

CHAPTER 30

CALEB

The shuttle arrived at noon the next day. Raphael set it down right next to our tank, and we spread out the huge solar blankets to augment the panels on the shuttle's top and recharge the power cores. The thrusters were driven by a small reactor, but the power cores handled the shuttle's life support system so that all the reactor's power went into the thruster engines.

We sat in the shade of the shuttle's wings, marveling at how well things had gone so far.

Josh leaned up against the shuttle's side. "Easy flight. Nirah's got this thing boosted up fast. Only took three hours to get here."

Raphael was checking the aft thrusters' attachment. "It'll probably take about eight to get to Horizon. Assuming we get out of atmosphere at all." He ran a hand through his shaggy brown hair. "Assuming we don't get melted by the blast."

Well, there was that.

Josh sighed. "Yeah. Not too excited about wearing a diaper under my suit. Not exactly the 'heroic astronaut' image I'm going for."

Raphael shrugged. "You get liquid floating around inside your suit, you'll be a lot less than heroic. Pee gets into the CO2 scrubber and you'll be dead."

They would be wearing full space suits for the entire flight. The shuttle was supposed to seal, and had its own oxygen system, but they wouldn't know if it could hold pressure until they left Ceti's surface. If it didn't, there wouldn't be time to put on helmets before they blacked out and died.

So many things could go wrong here.

Later in the afternoon, Josh wanted to climb up the caldera to see the bomb down in the hole. He and I made the ascent together, and perched on the inner ledge, our feet hanging over the edge.

"Doesn't look like much," he said, gazing down at the tiny metal cube far below us.

"Nope," I agreed. "Might not even work."

We sat in silence for a few minutes, gritty wind blowing around the backs of our necks.

"I'm really sorry about Erik. I know he was your best friend."

Josh nodded. "We survived a long time out there, just him and me. I got him through a gunshot in the middle of the scatting jungle."

I looked over at him and saw his cheeks were wet. He didn't wipe the tears away, just let them fall. They dried quickly in the hot breeze.

"We've just lost so many people." His voice was thick. "But we're not going to lose Dad. Or anybody else up there."

Behind and below us, Adam and Raphael were starting to pull in the solar blankets. First thing in the morning we would drive the tank a couple of kilometers away and send the detonation signal. As soon as the shuttle was safely on its way, we would start the six-day journey back to Carthage. If all went well, the shuttle would have made its journey and beat us back home.

"Just in case, though," Josh said, "take care of Mom and Malia, okay?"

My stomach turned at his words. We both knew how ridiculously dangerous this flight was. I didn't want to hear him say it.

"Yeah. I will. But it's gonna be fine. Nirah knows what she's doing."

We could hear her voice from below us, talking to Raphael, but they were too far away to make out any of the words. All of this was her plan. Mayor Borin hadn't wanted her to go on the flight, but she wouldn't hear of letting other people take the risk without her.

The wall of shadow crept over the bottom of the caldera, and we couldn't see the bomb anymore.

"Probably better get back down there," I said.

We descended in silence.

The sun was just crested over the horizon when we said our final goodbyes. I helped Josh struggle into his space suit, latching the helmet tight against the collar. He breathed deeply, the thick glass fogging and clearing with every breath. They all checked each other's suits, testing the communication system and CO_2 exchange. I had hugged Josh long and hard before he got all suited up, knowing it would be impossible once he was in the awkward equipment.

We stood facing each other, eyes locked together.

Don't cry. Josh isn't crying.

He held up a hand, palm facing me inside his thick white glove, and I placed my palm against his for a long minute until I heard Raphael's voice from the comm inside Josh's helmet.

"All right, team. Let's fly."

He gave me a tiny smile, turned away, and lumbered into the shuttle. The huge door closed with a squeal of metal, and my brother was gone.

A hand clapped onto my shoulder.

"Let's get moving," Shiro said. "Gotta get him up in the sky."

I couldn't look at my friend. It would be all over if I did. Shiro understood. He always did.

We climbed onto the tank and rumbled away from the caldera.

A few minutes later we stopped. Adam popped the hatch and we three sat on top.

"Shuttle One, do you copy?"

A staticky voice affirmed. "We copy. Ready for liftoff."

There was nothing but desert between us and the shuttle, and we watched it take off. It circled above the caldera, flew up and over our heads and hovered there, awaiting our signal that the detonation code had been sent.

"We ready for this?" Adam held the sat trans.

"Let me do it," I answered, and held out my hand for the trans.

He looked at me for a moment, then nodded. "Get in here as soon as you send."

Shiro and Adam joined Don inside the tank. I perched on the edge of the hatch, fingers trembling on the keypad.

Number by number, I punched it in.

"Shuttle One, we have sent the code. Detonation in two minutes."

I didn't wait for a reply, but scuttled down the ladder and pulled the hatch closed behind me.

Inside we all huddled against the tiny window. The shuttle would wait until twenty seconds before detonation, then zoom over the caldera, heading straight up, waiting for the blast to shoot them skyward.

Sixty seconds.

Fifty.

Forty.

Thirty seconds.

We couldn't see up into the air, but the edge of the caldera was in sight. We would see the explosion from inside the tank.

Twenty.

The shuttle's engines roared from its launch point.

Ten.

I was shaking as we counted down the final seconds. Overhead, the shuttle's rumble vibrated right through the tank.

Three.

Two.

One.

I squinted my eyes against the expected blast.

Nothing.

No explosion. And no shuttle at the edge to ride the lift of a blast that didn't happen.

"What's wrong?" I whispered to Don. "Did you calculate wrong?"

"No way," he said. "Nirah did the math. Two minutes from signal to detonation."

We waited another full minute.

Finally I couldn't stand it any longer. I popped the top of the tank and scrambled out.

The shuttle was still hovering overhead. They hadn't gotten the signal to fly. Neither had the bomb. I pulled out my sat trans and stared at the screen.

No satellite coverage. The Horizon array was down again, and without it, there was no way to detonate the explosion.

CHAPTER 31

CALEB

I ran out onto the desert and waved my arms. After a few minutes, the shuttle landed next to me and its door squealed open. Josh struggled out the hatch.

"What happened? Why didn't you launch?"

I pointed at my trans. "No satellite. No bomb. No launch."

"Oh for . . ." Josh stepped off the shuttle, grumbling. "How long 'till it comes back?"

Shiro appeared from behind me. "No way to know. Last time it went down, it took a week to come back up. Who knows what they had to do to fix it up there."

"Well, when will another satellite be overhead?" Josh glanced up at the sky.

Nirah stepped out of the shuttle. "It won't. Horizon is our main communication satellite. Coverage should be fine this far south." She grabbed the trans from my hand but couldn't operate it in her thick gloves. "It's on Horizon's end. And if they don't fix it, there's nothing we can do about it."

We waited all day.

And all the next day.

Does Horizon even realize they're down? They fixed it once. Can they fix it again? Nobody on Ceti had any idea.

At the end of the second day, we all sat inside the shuttle.

"We need another solution," Josh said.

I shook my head. "They'll get it fixed. They know what we're doing here. I'm sure they're working on it right now."

Nirah sighed. "I'm sure they are. Assuming they have what they need to fix it. Assuming it's fixable. But how long can we wait?"

We all looked out the open shuttle door. Tau Ceti d was clearly visible in the western sky. It was the equinox. The half moon was rising. More than half moon. And when the moon was full, the Flood would begin. We had a week.

"We can't wait," Nirah said. "We have to figure out another way."

I thought for a few moments.

"Can't we set a timer on the sat trans that's wired to the bomb? Set it to go off in, what, an hour? Two? Give us time to climb up and out before it goes off?"

Nirah shook her head. "I wouldn't trust the synchronization without any communication. If we were off by ten seconds, we could miss the detonation. Or worse, be right at the edge and get blown out sideways. Not even Raphael could steer that." She closed her eyes. "No, we can't have that much time for error. Even the two minutes to melt the wires is pushing it."

"Two minutes," Shiro muttered. "Two minutes." He sighed and looked up the hill. "What if the tank was parked right at the bottom? Would it survive the blast?"

Don stared at him. "Yes. Probably. As long as the rock density is what we think it is. But we're not going to be parked right at the bottom."

Shiro nodded. "Yes, you are. Nirah, can we reprogram the sat trans so that instead of sending a signal to detonate, it's sending a signal to not detonate?"

She cocked her head. "Sure. But what do you . . . oh." She nodded along with him. "Yes. I can do that."

I looked at Adam who shrugged.

"How does that help?" I asked.

Nirah ignored me, still focused on Shiro. "We set it to a stop signal. And we wire in a second trans between the stop signal and the detonator. When the second trans loses that stop signal, it will default to go. Destroy one, and use the second one to power the charge."

I still had no idea what they meant.

Shiro was still looking up the hill. "It's simple. We hook two sat trans together. One says stop, and the other says go. We destroy the one saying 'stop,' and what's left is . . ."

"Go," I finished. "And how are we going to destroy the one saying 'stop?'"

"We shoot it from the top of the ridge."

Shiro was the best marksman. I argued for an hour that it should be me, but there was no denying that he was the best shot. Two minutes. From the time he made the hit, destroying the correct sat trans, he'd have two minutes to get down the hill and get inside the tank before the whole world exploded.

He thought he could make the climb. I knew there was no way. He'd die on that hillside. He probably knew it too. That's who Shiro was.

The zip line was my idea.

We hauled the cable back up to the rock and secured the hook around it. Adam drove the tank just far enough away to pull the line taut, making a terrifyingly steep zip line from the rock down to the tank.

He had one chance.

Once again, we said goodbye to the flight crew. I didn't know who I was more worried about—Josh or Shiro.

I watched the shuttle take off and circle to its runway distance.

Adam and Don were inside the tank. I stood at the front where the winch attached to the cable.

I watched Shiro at the top of the hill, so far away.

He was already attached to the line. He crouched on the edge and brought the rifle to his shoulder. It bucked once and I tensed. Nothing. Miss.

It bucked again and he jumped up, waving the rifle over his head, the signal to the shuttle that the sat trans was hit.

Two minutes.

He leaped into the air and flew down the line.

Ninety seconds.

The cable shrieked as the metal ring zipped down its length.

Sixty seconds.

He plowed into me at the bottom and I helped him rip off the rope harness that held him onto the cable.

Thirty seconds.

We bolted up the side of the tank just as the shuttle roared overhead.

Twenty seconds.

Shiro dropped in.

Ten seconds.

I dropped in and slammed the hatch closed over my head.

Three.

Two.

One.

The tank rocked with the force of the blast, lifting off its treads and slamming into the ground. The sound was indescribable.

We couldn't see through the windows and we couldn't pop the hatch. There was no communication.

We sat in the dark inside the tank, hoping the shuttle had made it.

CHAPTER 32

JOSH

I was pretty sure the blast was going to kill us. And I didn't much care. My best friend, whose calm, sane voice kept me alive through three hopeless months in that tiny cave, fell down a flight of alien-carved stairs and died. After all the dangers we faced, that stupid accident was more than I could take. I should have been there with him. I could have caught him when he fell. But I wasn't, and he died, so now I was sitting in a hovering shuttle, waiting to fly straight into a nuclear explosion that was as likely to melt our ship as it was to shove us skyward. At least no one else would die with us. Nirah came up with the plan and accepted the risk, and Raphael was always a loose cannon, which was why he was our best pilot. So we hovered and waited for the signal.

Raphael sat in the pilot's chair, and I sat next to him. We both saw Shiro's signal at the same moment. He said, "That's it, he made the shot."

Nirah was seated just behind us. We had left enough seats on the shuttle for us and all the survivors on Horizon, and had plenty of room in the back for the cargo we hoped to return with. I turned around and saw her tugging on her seat harness, struggling with the straps in her thick gloves.

"All right." Her voice was like ice. "We fly in ninety seconds."

The minute and a half took a lifetime as we watched Shiro slide down the zip line to the tank.

"And here we go." Raphael gunned the thrusters and we shot forward toward the caldera.

He angled steeply upward and I lost sight of the tank through the windshield. I couldn't see Shiro make his landing, or if he and Caleb were scrambling into the tank. *Get in there, guys. Nobody else needs to die.*

We shot out over the pit and Raphael punched it straight up. My stomach was left behind, G-forces squashing me into my seat.

The nuke exploded.

I felt the shuttle lurch as the first wave of force hit us from below. We were flipped upwards like a tossed coin. My brain went fuzzy, and all I could see was blue sky overhead. None of us were talking and I couldn't even turn my head to see if Raphael was conscious.

The thrusters screamed.

And the sky got darker.

I still couldn't move my arms, but somehow Raphael still had his hands on the ship's controls. He was giving it everything the little shuttle had to get us into the stratosphere.

My arms got lighter and the heaviness in my stomach was replaced with a strange, yawning feeling.

"Yes! Goodbye, Ceti!" Raphael was screaming into the comm.

The seat harness held me in place, but all around me the air in the shuttle was filled with floating debris. Every speck of dust, every hair, every tiny leaf and lost screw from the repair was suddenly freed from gravity, floating around the shuttle's interior.

"Josh, how's our pressure holding?"

I blinked. Oh, yeah. That was my job. The instrument panel before me was flashing with a hundred different numbers. I tried to remember which screen I was supposed to be looking at.

"Josh? Report now!"

That one.

"So far so good," I said. We weren't going to test it by taking off our helmets, but if the shuttle was tight and we were able to seal onto a portion of Horizon that still had normal pressure, we could take off these blasted suits while we were inside.

We're going to make it. We actually survived that launch and we're going to make it.

The sky was black, with a million stars. While we were shooting skyward, we were heading away from the sun, which would rise and set as we orbited, heading for Horizon Alpha. I couldn't turn far enough around to see out any of the back windows where Ceti's surface would be vanishing into the distance.

"Everybody okay?" Raphael didn't take his eyes off the instruments before him.

"It worked," Nirah murmured from the seat behind me. Her voice echoed straight into my head through the comm system. "It actually worked."

Please, please, please, let Caleb and Shiro have gotten into the tank in time. I wouldn't know until we landed back in Carthage, and a million things could go wrong between now and then.

I remembered this weightless feeling from my childhood. The spinning cylinders of Horizon Alpha gave us a false gravity, but the central tube around which they spun was always weightless. We weren't supposed to play up there, but of course we did, bouncing around from wall to wall. I had the urge to unfasten my seat harness and float through the shuttle, but there was so much garbage drifting around the interior that I didn't dare. If any of the junk got stuck in a vital crevasse in the ship, we could be in major trouble. So I sat there, marveling at the stars. On Ceti, the nights were dark enough to see a galaxy full, but out here without the interference of the atmosphere, the view was breathtaking. Just like I remembered from all those years on Horizon.

"Should be about two hours until we're in position to attempt a docking." Raphael checked the satellite again, but there was nothing from Horizon Alpha. "Assuming there's anyone there to meet us."

But of course there would be. We hadn't gone through all this, risked and lost so many lives just to arrive at a dead ship. Dad was there. And all the others. Unless something happened. Unless they lost life support somehow. Even if they did, we had a job to do.

It wasn't just the weightlessness that made my stomach turn over. Every life in Carthage depended on the success of this mission. We had to get home with the equipment. Mom and Malia and baby Teddy . . . They were all down there waiting, not knowing if we'd survived the launch, wondering if we were coming home with the equipment that would keep them safe when the Flood came. If we failed, all of them could die.

"They're up there," I said. "We'll get them, and bring them home."

CHAPTER 33

JOSH

The Horizon Alpha was a mess.

We approached her from the starboard side, and the damage from the fires was heartbreaking. The ship was constructed with three huge cylinders that spun around a central axis. All three were separate, but should have been spinning in synchrony, creating the gravity I'd known for the first fifteen years of my life. Now Tubes One and Two were still. Tube Three still spun on its own, but the glittering lights that should have shown from a thousand tiny portholes were dark.

Most of Tube One was destroyed by the fire. Charred, black holes pocked the surface. Horizon Alpha, humanity's crowning achievement, was a derelict husk limping through the night sky.

"I'm going underneath, see if we can see the satellite array." Raphael maneuvered our shuttle to aim it below Horizon's huge round belly.

The satellite array should have been on the aft portion of the central axis, pointing straight at Ceti. I had seen it when we evacuated the ship three years ago, and it looked like some crazy metal plant with huge leaves sticking off a central attachment. Now there was nothing. As we moved in closer, I could see what was left of the thick metal post that had supported the communication system. It stuck out from the ship's tail with nothing left of its array.

"It's gone. All of it's gone." I said it mostly for Nirah, who probably couldn't see through the front screen from her seat behind me.

Up close, the ship looked even worse. Two hundred years of space travel had taken a toll. Every metal surface was scratched and dented from millions of tiny impacts along the way. The pictures we had seen of Horizon's exterior were all from the days when she was brand new, before our ancestors ever left Earth's solar system. Back then she was sleek and gorgeous, a great shining city in the beauty of space. Now she was old and scarred, gasping for her final breaths in orbit around a planet of death.

"What a beauty," Raphael said, and I craned in my seat to stare at him. Were we looking at the same thing? But his eyes were wide as he gazed at Horizon.

Nirah's voice held the same awe. "She got us here. The builders would have been so proud."

I looked back at the ship as we passed underneath the tail. To our port side, Tube Three rotated slowly. One of the sections was still lit, though we couldn't see anything through the tiny windows. *She got us here. And we're still fighting.*

Once, on a mission, I had seen a very old Brachi with her family. We were out in the tank, and the noise of our approach startled them across a wide field. Her skin was covered in deep puckered scars and she walked with a pronounced limp in her right front leg. Half of her tail was missing. But she had two babies capering at her sides. A smaller carnivore was taking advantage of our noise. It wasn't as big as a Rex, and it had a sharp horn on the front of its nose. It lunged at one of the babies.

The mangled mama Brachi whipped around, whacking that 'saur with the stump of her tail. She caught it right in the leg and although we couldn't hear it snap, the attacking 'saur went down inches from the baby. Mama trampled it, stomping until the 'saur was a pile of mush. She flicked that tail and led her babies off into the trees.

Horizon reminded me of that mama Brachi. Ugly and broken, but still fighting for her children.

"Approaching Dock Six." Raphael had flown us around to the front and was maneuvering us into position.

All the shuttle docks were on the static central axis, since even Raphael couldn't hope to dock a ship on a spinning cylinder. Our relative speeds made it look like Horizon wasn't moving, but in reality both she and our shuttle were blasting around the planet at about four thousand meters per second. Raphael had once described docking a shuttle as "jumping off the back of a flying pterosaur and landing on the back of a running Wolf."

A thought struck me, and I couldn't believe I'd never considered it already. "You've never actually done this before, have you?"

Raphael was focused on the docking bay, which looked ridiculously tiny. "I did it a thousand times in the simulator on board Horizon."

"Right." My mouth was dry from the recycled air in my suit. "That was three years ago."

"That's right, Josh," Raphael said. "So please shut up and let me fly."

I shut up.

Each docking port was an oval-shaped metal ring on the side of Horizon. They had robotic metal arms that were supposed to reach out and lock onto an attachment on the side of a shuttle and reel it in to meet the ring. The ring would lock around the ship and we'd be solidly attached.

Inside the port was an anteroom where the ship would test for pressure, making sure there were no leaks from the join. That process was supposed to take about an hour. Then the inner door would open and we'd open our shuttle hatch, and float on into the central axis of Horizon.

We moved into position next to the port. When we still had satellite contact, we had agreed on Dock Six. But there had been no contact for two days now. They couldn't even know we were coming.

"So what happens if they can't run the robot arm?"

Nirah answered me. "It's possible for us to dock ourselves. The shuttle has a remote control that should allow us to open both hatches from inside here."

"Assuming we can get ourselves situated in the ring." I looked at Raphael, focused on his instrument panel.

"Raphael can do it."

Nirah's confidence was not contagious. At least, not to me. But I didn't matter.

"Of course he can," I said for his benefit.

He didn't seem to appreciate the gesture. "Will you both please just shut up and let me do this?" It was cold in the shuttle, but sweat was beading on his forehead inside his helmet.

The robot arm was supposed to extend from a little port on the side of the large ring. Raphael kept the shuttle right next to Horizon and we waited.

And waited.

The arm wasn't coming.

Finally I couldn't stand it. "How long do we give them? Do we even know they're alive in there?"

Nobody answered. We waited.

Time slowed to a crawl. It might have been only minutes, but it felt like hours as we hung there with Horizon's huge metal bulk out the port side windows and the blackness of space out the starboard side.

The arm extended.

"Yes! They're here!" I pumped my fist, and debris swirled in the air around my helmet.

We felt the clunk as the arm latched onto our side, and Horizon got closer and closer until it was close enough to touch. The shuttle vibrated when the docking ring closed around it, locking us onto the ship's side.

"And now we wait. Once they're sure the pressure is holding, they'll open up from their side."

Horizon lay between us and Ceti, so I couldn't see the planet spinning below us. I settled in for a long, boring hour.

Five minutes later I jumped at a loud metal squeal. "What was that? Are we still attached?"

Our shuttle's hatch opened from the outside. I ripped off my harness and shoved myself back into the main compartment, pushing Nirah out of my way as I went.

There, in the middle of the two open hatches, a figure floated in an exposure suit.

I pushed off the shuttle's seats and spun into an awkward spacesuit hug with my dad.

CHAPTER 34

JOSH

It took a couple of minutes for us to get on the same comm frequency so we could talk to each other. That was mostly because Dad was crying inside his helmet and couldn't work the controls on the front of his suit, which required using the little mirror mounted on the forearm. We were ungainly hulks in those suits, but this part of Horizon was obviously depressurized, so there was no taking off our helmets for a conversation.

His first words to me in three years were, "I'm so proud of you, son."

It got a little harder for me to work my own controls after that.

He and Nirah fell into quick conversation and we learned that the whole satellite array had been taken out a few days ago by a meteoroid, one of the little rocks whizzing around the planet, held by its gravity. Life support and pressurization was fine in Tube Three, where the other ten survivors were waiting for us to arrive.

"I have to admit," Dad said to Nirah, "I really didn't think you'd make it. We knew you were trying, but with no communication at all, we had no idea if you'd managed the launch, or survived it. We've been taking shifts at the dock for the last two days just in case you came knocking at our door. I've never been happier to see anyone in my life."

The ship's interior was dark, and we relied on the lights on our helmets to maneuver down the long corridor. There was no gravity in this section, and we all pushed off the walls, bouncing toward the back of the ship. Rows of speakers ripped from the walls—along with carefully bundled coils of wire—lined the sides, held in place by nets so they didn't float around.

"We got everything together." Dad checked each net as we drifted by. "Based on our calculations, this should circle the whole valley. Plenty of wire so we don't have to rely on wireless interface, though we'll have that as a backup."

The next net held crates that were of distinct interest to me. Weapons. Welding torches. A whole crate of sat trans, which wouldn't be very useful since Horizon's array was permanently offline, but we had already found a lot of other uses for them. Medical equipment that Mom had been pining for. More seeds, frozen from Earth. And a giant bag labeled "Boots," which would be very welcome on a planet where we had been forced to tan the hides of 'saurs for the strange leather they gave us.

This part of the ship had always been used for storage since it never had gravity. My stomach was queasy watching my crew mates pulling themselves along the walls, floor, and ceiling of the hallway. Up and down made no difference up here, and there was as much equipment attached directly over my head as there was on the sides. With only the light from my helmet, I was quickly disoriented. It felt like we were at the bottom of a deep well, pulling ourselves upward and I had to keep reminding myself to breathe normally and not gasp for air.

Finally we arrived at a hatchway and Dad pulled it open. We piled inside and closed the door behind us. He hit a lever on the wall and a screen lit up, counting down as the little chamber pressurized. After about ten minutes, the red numbers turned green, and the door to the pressurized section of Horizon opened automatically. There was still no gravity, but after we passed through the hatchway we were able to pull off our helmets.

I had forgotten what Horizon smelled like. Three years in the fresh, green air of Ceti wiped the stale, dead smell of this ship from my mind. Faintly metallic, the air was still and old. The carbon dioxide was higher in the ship, and my head immediately started throbbing as I breathed in oxygen that had been recycled and recycled for two hundred years.

"You're not going to believe how good it feels to breathe Ceti air," I said to Dad, and he smiled.

"I can't even imagine. And to eat fresh food . . . fruit and meat . . ." He shook his head. "I truly can't imagine. Do you remember when you first tasted real food?"

I did. At the time I didn't even have words for the sweetness of actual planet-grown fruit.

Dad led us down the corridor. "We've been living in Tube Three since the evacuation. There are eleven of us left. I thought we'd go down and get the others, and let you guys rest for a little while before we took off. I doubt you'll want to eat any algae paste or drink our filtered water, but it's all we have to offer. We only heat and light the couple of rooms we live in to save power. At least the bathroom facility still works."

Nirah had a large bag attached to the belt of her suit and it floated along next to her. I knew what she'd brought, and couldn't wait for her to open it.

We pulled ourselves into a small, square room, and used the handholds on the walls to maneuver into seats and belt ourselves in. The seats felt to my perspective like they were on the right hand wall, but I had ridden in these elevators a million times as a kid. It was best to close my eyes, but this time I didn't.

"Everybody in?" Dad reached up to the control panel.

We all nodded and he hit the button. The doors closed and the room gave a lurch. It slid along the wide top of what would become an elevator shaft and locked into place. As we descended, gravity reasserted itself little by little. The whole shaft was rotating as part of the huge cylinder, and the sense of movement made my stomach turn again. At least if I threw up now, it wouldn't end up inside my helmet.

Nirah didn't make it. She grabbed one of the bags helpfully attached under the seats and lost her lunch with a great heave.

Oh boy. Didn't need to smell that.

I held on somehow, feeling my body get heavier as we descended to the outer level of the spinning tube. For the first fifteen years of my life, this had been normal to me, this constant movement. I hadn't even realized it. Now I was aware of the constant slow spin. I needed to go to the bathroom, but other than that, the sooner we were off this puke factory, the better.

Dad just kept looking at me. He didn't look much different than he had the last time I saw him. A little older, and a little thinner, but still just Dad. I must look very different to him, though. Bigger and stronger. A man now, and not just a teenager.

Everyone was waiting when the elevator doors opened. They were all in the soft brown clothing we had worn in the temperature-controlled environment. They looked pale and sallow. Had we looked like this when we landed? Of course we had. Our skin had never seen sunshine. Our lungs had never breathed fresh air.

Aunt Marci was the first to throw her arms around me. "Josh, you're so big! I can't believe you're really here!" I'd never thought Ryenne looked like her mom before, but she'd grown to resemble her so much in the last few years. Marci would be so proud of her daughter and her "grandbaby" 'saurs.

Bethany was next. She hugged me from the side, careful not to squash any of the controls on the chest of the spacesuit I still wore. "You're a sight for sore eyes," she said, and her eyes did look sore, red-rimmed with happy tears. "Can't even believe my dad's crazy bomb got you all the way up here." She grinned. "He always drove me crazy, my whole life. But I sure can't wait to see him."

We stripped out of our suits between hugs and raced for the bathrooms. I hadn't been too excited about wearing a diaper for this trip, and had somehow managed to hold it all these hours.

Everything looked so small, so old and dirty and dark. All the survivors had gathered in what used to be a common room with couches and readers and video players. It had seemed huge when I was a kid, one of the few really open spaces on a ship built for efficiency. Now I had my own room in the cave that was almost as big as this, all to myself. That thought brought heat to my face again. No roommate to go home to after this mission. I spent a few minutes in the bathroom splashing old water on my face before returning to the others.

When I got back to the common room where everyone was still hugging each other and laughing and crying, Nirah was ready to open the bag she'd brought.

The Horizon crews' eyes were as big as the round yellow fruits she pulled out of the sack.

"We thought we should have one last snack on Horizon." She removed a knife from the inside pocket of her undersuit and cut off bite-sized chunks, handing them to each person. "Here you go. Your first taste of Tau Ceti e."

Bethany slurped at the fruit, her eyes almost crossing with pleasure. "I had no idea anything could ever taste like this."

I thought they were all going to dissolve into little puddles of joy right there on the floor.

"Just you all wait," I said. "With a little luck, we'll be home in time for breakfast."

CHAPTER 35

CALEB

We left the desert behind us and rumbled back into the jungle, heading for home. The tank was dark and smelly, and not knowing if the shuttle had even survived that launch made us all edgy and tense.

Did they make it?

If they did, was Horizon intact when they got there?

Are any of them alive?

Adam was driving, his legs tucked up under the front window. Don slept in the seat behind him, having driven all the night before, and Shiro and I were in the rear. The noise of the engine made it hard to talk, and I was just as glad not to. We left the top open for some air, and I watched the tree canopy creep by overhead.

Don stirred in the seat in front of me, and tapped Adam on the shoulder. "Hey, need to make a pit stop."

When we had to stop in daylight, we stayed close to the tank, doing our business as fast as possible. I climbed the hot metal ladder and popped out the top to look around while we were still moving, glad for the fresh air. The jungle was dense here. Adam was following the path we broke on our way down, already growing over in a week's time. There was room for us to get out on the sides, but not much. Fortunately, we had all grown adept at kneeling on the back of the tank, watering the crushed foliage behind us when we needed to. We didn't usually have to stop at all. But none of us were able to do more than water, so when it was fertilizer time, whoever had to go would jump down. I always held it until nightfall if I could.

The tank slowed to a stop and I waited, peering at every leaf, every bush. Anything could be hiding no more than a few feet away. The loud calls of the little tree 'saurs overhead reassured me that nothing huge was nearby. But the canopy-dwellers wouldn't care about a Gila or a Wolf on the ground.

After a few long minutes, I climbed the rest of the way out, making room for Don to come up behind me.

"Stay in sight, and be quick," I warned him.

He blinked at me. "I'm not staying in sight."

Stars. I don't need this now. "I won't watch. But it's daytime. Anything could be out there."

A couple of little 'saurs trundled over the path behind us, barely glancing at the huge tank idling just meters away. They weren't afraid of our noise out here. Death in the jungle was never announced loudly. It came on silent feet.

Don climbed off the back of the tank and followed the little 'saurs off the path.

"Get back here," I hissed from the top of the tank, but he ignored me.

Scat him. He's going to get himself killed out here. If something found him in the leaves, I'd never get there in time. I pulled out my pistol, but I couldn't see him through the dense foliage. If he was attacked, I wouldn't know where to shoot.

The bushed moved where he'd disappeared and my heart leaped into my throat. I raised my pistol, searching for a shape to focus on.

A scream from the bushes.

Human.

Scat him.

Don burst out of the brush, pants around his ankles. He tripped and fell flat on his face, and I trained the pistol on the spot where he'd just emerged.

Then the smell hit me, a putrid odor that reminded me of dead fish I'd smelled long ago on the beach where Transport Seventeen crashed. I had smelled it before, back at Eden Base, but I didn't know what dead fish smelled like back then.

They smelled like this.

Don's backside was splattered with brown, sticky oil that reeked straight up to the stars.

. "So those little 'saurs that just went by?" I began, eyes watering at the stench. "You don't wanna scare them. They've got some kind of scent gland they spray when they're scared." *Idiot. Probably tried to touch one*

Don hiked his pants up and scrambled for the back of the tank. I hopped back into the hatch, blocking it with my body. "No way you're getting in here with that all over you."

He sputtered, trying to push his way in. "Those things . . . I wasn't even . . ."

"Nope." I shoved him away and backed down the ladder until only my head was out. "We'll find someplace you can wash off tonight. Hunker down under the gun. You'll be safe enough."

He lunged at the hatch as I pulled it almost closed. "You can't leave me out here!"

I grinned out at him. "You'll be fine. Smelling like that, you're the safest thing in the jungle."

I flipped the lock on the hatch, leaving him cursing on top of the tank.

CHAPTER 36

JOSH

Nobody wanted to stay an extra minute on Horizon. Once the fruit was all gone and everyone had licked their fingers clean, we struggled back into our spacesuits for the return trip. I noticed that the Horizon crew's suits all hung loosely on their skinny bodies, while ours were a lot more filled out. None of us were fat, but the extra muscle we'd gained from a few years in stronger gravity with ample fresh food and a ton of exercise made an obvious difference.

"So here are your assignments," Dad said, glancing at the timepiece on his suit's left arm. "Nirah, Josh, and Raphael, you'll take everyone but me and Bethany up to the equipment we packed and start loading it into the shuttle." His face grew somber. "Horizon is on its last legs. We're losing altitude because everything is starting to break down without maintenance up here. It's far too dangerous to just let her fall when she's ready."

I had wondered about that. A ship the size of Horizon would make a huge crater if it fell onto land. And if it fell anywhere near our valley, it could kick up a dust cloud that might be the end of our whole species. We were supposed to control Horizon's eventual descent via the satellites, and that was obviously not going to happen.

"Bethany and I will initiate the destruction sequence that will break the ship into pieces when it hits the atmosphere. Once we're all on board the shuttle, we'll use its thrusters to push the ship down. Bethany's done all the calculations. It won't take much to alter the trajectory so that Horizon will go down on the opposite side of the planet from Carthage, and land in the ocean. We'll be cutting it a little bit close, but once we get Horizon moving in the right direction, we'll be able to undock and fly back to our own re-entry site. The shuttle's been charging since it docked, so we should have no problem getting down to the valley."

Raphael and I glanced at each other. Dad was right that we'd have no trouble getting down to the valley. But he hadn't been on any of our landing craft the first time we left this ship. Getting down was easy. Gravity would make sure of that. Making another safe landing with a shuttle packed full of people and equipment . . . My stomach twisted, and not from hunger.

No reason to wait, though. It wouldn't get any easier the longer we stayed up here. And the constant spinning motion of the ship was not something I'd miss when we left.

We all checked each other's suits, and piled into the elevator. There were two separation points built into Horizon's hull, places where a couple of planned charges would break the ship into three large pieces. That was all planned by the designers who knew she might someday have to be broken up for a planned crash into the planet's surface. They tried to think of everything. Dad and Bethany would wait at those detonators until we had everything loaded up. We had the comm system working helmet-to-helmet, so as soon as all the equipment was secured and the passengers belted in, they would initiate the sequence. Thirty minutes later, the ship would blow. By then, the shuttle would have pushed it into a downward trajectory using Bethany's calculations to ensure atmospheric entry and eventual crash into the ocean on the far side of the planet from Carthage. Dad and Bethany would have plenty of time to get to the shuttle so we could undock and fly away before gravity grabbed hold of us.

We got lighter and lighter as the elevator neared the central hub, and my stomach grew more and more rebellious. Finally I heard and felt the clunk of the elevator car disengaging from the spinning shaft, and my body was weightless again. I was the first one out of the car and into the central axis corridor.

"Okay, everybody, here we go," I said, pushing off the wall to shoot myself forward down the hallway. The first separation point was close to the elevator entry, and we left Bethany there. She grabbed a handhold next to the large metal breaker box that held the keypad which would initiate the sequence.

"Don't take too long. I'm ready to blow this thing. I need more of that fruit." She spun in lazy cartwheels as we all filed away from her.

We left my dad at the second breaker box. He opened the door and powered up the keypad, hooking his foot under one of the many metal bars attached along the walls for that purpose. "Let us know when you're all set."

I didn't want to leave him there, didn't want to let him out of my sight. But that was silly. We were only heading farther down the long, dark corridor to where he had carefully organized all the things we were packing down on this final journey from the ship. *Just get us loaded up. Plenty of time to be with Dad once we're safely on the ground.* As if the ground was actually safe.

Nirah was taking charge of the loading process. We had just enough seats on the shuttle for everyone to belt in, and the rest of the room was for cargo. Everything had to be attached with nets or stowed in bags because gravity would soon grab us hard, and anything not secured would rattle around in the back, which could throw off the shuttle's balance. I trusted Raphael to land us safely, but we had to be sure not to make his job any harder.

I supervised the unloading, helping everyone to unhook whatever they were trying to maneuver down the corridor and through the entry hatch. We took the most sensitive medical equipment first so it didn't get banged up by other crates going by. Everything was weightless, but once a box or bag got moving, there was nothing to stop it. Guiding the larger pieces of equipment was a four-person job, making sure nothing hit the walls or got hung up on anything else.

We loaded the sound equipment next, then the weapons, seeds, and other miscellaneous boxes of things Dad had thought would be most useful to us in the valley. Finally the long hallway was stripped bare, and I pulled the last crate along with me as I entered the shuttle.

Nirah had everything well strapped down in the back, and was starting to help get all the people into their seats. I stuffed my crate into a net of other crates, and clamped down the free edge to a ring on the floor. Re-entry would be a bumpy ride, but everything looked secure.

We left the copilot's seat next to Raphael open for Dad. I strapped into the seat nearest the shuttle's open door, and Raphael made the call.

"Horizon Crew, shuttle is secure. Ready to initiate thrusters."

Dad's voice echoed in my helmet. "Roger that, Shuttle. Ready to initiate separation sequence. Bethany?"

And then Bethany. "Roger that, Captain. Ready to initiate separation sequence."

"Shuttle, engage thrusters."

The shuttle roared to life. One worry down. A tiny part of me had been terrified that it wouldn't start.

"Horizon Crew, we have begun our push. Time to Horizon's atmosphere burn, thirty minutes."

"Roger that. Bethany, on my mark, initiate separation. Three. Two. One. Go."

There was no blaring warning, no emergency voice. All the speakers that should have been screaming that the ship was going to blow in half an hour were safely stowed in the cargo area behind my seat.

Even over the roar of the thrusters, I could hear my own heartbeat. Or maybe I just felt it pounding in my ears. Our little shuttle was pushing the great ark Horizon into its final dive. A two-hundred-year voyage was less than an hour from a fiery crash into a dinosaur-filled ocean.

I didn't realize I was holding my breath until it whooshed out of me in a huge sigh when the space-suited shape of my father filled the hatchway. He pulled himself through the door and gave me a thumbs-up as he passed my seat on his way to the cockpit.

We waited for Bethany.

She didn't come.

"Bethany, report your location." Dad sounded worried.

It took a moment before her voice responded over the comm. "On my way, Captain. I'm hung up in one of the nets."

"Do you require assistance?"

"Negative, Captain. I'm almost free."

We waited, and it felt like hours. I could hear my breathing inside my helmet. It was thirty minutes to re-entry from the time they initiated the sequence. Which meant twenty minutes until we needed to be undocked and on our way.

"Bethany?"

"Almost there, Captain."

Finally she appeared. She used the manual lever to close the Horizon-side portal to the decompression bay that separated the shuttle from the hull of the ship. The shuttle side would close automatically when we undocked, not that it would matter in another fifteen minutes or so.

Bethany closed the shuttle's hatch and pulled herself over me. I helped her buckle into the seat next to me.

"All clear, Captain. All secure."

"Roger that. Two minutes to shuttle release."

I counted down in my head. Raphael would control the release timing from the cockpit. We would watch Horizon fall away from us as we turned toward our own re-entry point, half a world away.

"Release in three. Two. One. Shuttle release."

There was a harsh grinding noise and I looked out the small window at the side of Horizon just a few meters away.

It didn't move.

"Second attempt, shuttle release."

This time we didn't even get the grinding noise.

Horizon Alpha was going down in a fiery crash straight into the ocean. And we were locked onto her side.

Voices erupted all around, filling my helmet with noise. I unbuckled my harness and met my dad at the hatch.

"Sit down, son. I'm going to see what's holding us up."

He pulled open the hatch and floated into the decompression bay, turning to examine the metal ring that kept our shuttle clamped onto Horizon's side. I wasn't sure how the attachment really worked but I could see daylight around the edges. The ring had obviously unclamped like it was supposed to.

"It's the arm. It's locked."

I pushed out to where Dad was holding onto the robotic arm that had reeled us in to dock.

"It's supposed to let go when the ring lets go." Dad glanced at the timer on his arm.

I didn't want to ask, but I had to know. "How long . . ."

"Four minutes," he grumbled. "We need to be clear of this thing in four minutes. Six at the outside."

My helmet was full of frightened murmurs from the people in the shuttle. It didn't help me concentrate.

"Why won't it unlock?" I grabbed at the arm and tugged on it but it was cold steel locked into place.

"Because this ship is two hundred years old," Dad said. He braced his feet against the side of the decompression bay and pulled on the arm, but it didn't budge. "Might have knocked into it while we were loading. Don't know."

Everyone had tried to be careful loading all the crates of stuff.

Crates of stuff.

One of those crates was full of metalworking supplies. Blowtorches.

"Dad, we can cut it free!" I pushed away from the hatch and shoved myself toward the cargo hold. *Where is it? Which box?* Everything was stacked and netted down. I grabbed at the netting.

"There's no time, son." Dad's voice was inside my helmet, but I ignored it, searching through the stacked boxes.

I kept pulling at the netting until I heard the shuttle's hatch close. By the time I spun around, it had sealed into place.

"No! Dad, No!" I left the cargo nets flapping free and lunged for the door.

Bethany grabbed my leg as I bounced into her. "Josh, you can't open it. We have to go. One more minute and we won't make it back." She held my leg and I pulled on the seat, straining to reach the hatch.

With a lurch and a clunk, the arm let go. I pressed my helmet up against the small window in the hatch.

Our shuttle floated free from Horizon. Dad had opened Horizon's inner bay door and was hanging in the doorway clutching onto the robot arm's manual release lever, his feet kicking out into empty space.

The comms still worked.

"Josh, you have to listen to me."

My ears were ringing and all I could hear was my Dad's voice.

"Josh, you have to take care of Randa. Take care of Malia and the baby. Tell Caleb I love him and I'm so proud of him. Josh, I'm so proud of you all."

He got smaller and smaller as the shuttle moved away from the falling spaceship. The comm started to break up, but I heard his final words.

"I'm going to try and get . . ." The comm cut out.

I banged my fist against the hatch, pounding on it until hands pulled me away. Someone wrestled me into my seat and someone else belted me in. The shuttle turned away from Horizon, disappearing into the darkening sky.

★ ★ ★

Raphael flew us away from the crashing mothership as fast as the thrusters would carry us. We didn't see Horizon separate into three useless hunks of metal. We didn't see her burn up as she fell into the atmosphere, nor her final flaming plunge into the sea. But that was all I could imagine as we flew away, leaving my Dad to go down with his ship.

Our windows filled with fire as we re-entered Ceti's atmosphere, and the shuttle bounced and shook in the sky. Finally the windows cleared and gravity grabbed hold of us. Everything in the cargo area settled to the ship's floor, and all the dust and floating debris dropped everywhere. It was going to be a tough landing with this much cargo.

How am I going to tell Caleb? There was nothing but emptiness inside me, nothing but the pounding of my head inside the helmet. Bethany kept trying to grab my hand, and her words rattled around in the echo of my helmet. Words meant nothing. I had left my dad to die again.

The shuttle was equipped with two huge emergency parachutes. Raphael deployed them and crates smashed to the floor as the chutes grabbed the air and arrested our fall. The plan was to float down on the parachutes for part of the drop to save the thrusters for our final approach.

I looked out the window at the surface of this scatting planet that had cost us so much. From up here, I could see the dark, rolling ridges of a mountain range. It crawled along the planet's surface looking like the back of some giant 'saur lying in wait for us to land.

With another lurch, the parachutes were released. Thrusters screamed as we raced for the ground. We had debated long and hard about where to land. If we set down in the middle of the valley, we would have the shuttle there and could lock the children and babies inside it when the Flood came, in case our grand idea with the speakers didn't work. But the mountains were so high that the landing would be incredibly risky. And once inside the valley, it would never leave.

No reason to. Nowhere to go.

The shuttle creaked and groaned and the ground loomed closer and closer.

"Brace for landing."

Those who had argued for leaving the shuttle outside the valley had won, and we were heading for the place we'd taken off from, just outside the entrance to the cave where I'd spent months keeping Erik alive after our failed mission in the jungle.

Why did I bother? I couldn't save him from a stupid fall on a stone staircase. And although I braved a nuclear explosion to fly into space, I couldn't save my dad either.

I was going to have to tell Mom and Caleb.

My hands felt like ice inside the thick gloves, and sweat poured down my back.

It should have been me.

The mountain rose up outside my window. *Too fast. Too fast.* The shoulder harness cut into my suit as we slammed into the ground and skidded across the dirt. When we finally stopped moving, Raphael's voice was the first thing I heard.

"Everyone all right back there?"

I sat back in my seat and reached for my harness. It was covered in blood.

My shoulders ached from the landing, and I ripped off my helmet and gloves, clawing myself free of the harness. My head was throbbing and everything hurt from the rough landing, but the blood wasn't mine.

A crate of weapons was spilled all over the cabin. It must have worked its way free of the netting. The netting I had left unclamped in my struggle to get to my dad.

The side of the crate was dented and bloody. Next to me Bethany was slumped forward in her seat, her helmet missing and the back of her head caved in.

I grabbed her shoulders and sat her upright, but I knew before I even saw her face.

Bethany Rand was dead.

★ ★ ★

We weren't much good at funerals. For all those years on Horizon, our people had a simple service, with loved ones sharing memories of the deceased as the body was delivered into the reclamation system that would recycle them into the basic components we all lived on. Since we had finally found safety in Carthage, we still tried to do the whole memory sharing thing. In our early days at Eden Base we had let it slide, as humans often became 'saur food in numbers larger than one.

But now we were attending our second funeral in two weeks.

We stood around the little patch we'd set aside to bury our dead, those whose bodies were available for such an honor. In the months we'd been here, we'd only buried a couple of people. I stood at the foot of Erik's fresh grave, the grass not even beginning to grow in over the mound of dirt we'd shoveled over his sheet-wrapped body. Bethany would be laid to rest right next to him.

I had dug her grave myself, laboring all night. Her father was somewhere in the jungle, rumbling back toward Eden in the tank with my brother. He wouldn't get to see his daughter's face. She had been so excited to see him. He had risked his life to rescue her, and now we had to bury her before he returned, because there was nowhere cool to store a body.

We had no set funeral text. The people who had been stuck on Horizon with her these past three years all spoke, sharing memories of her on the ship.

Aunt Marci spoke last. "Bethany wanted so badly to see this planet. Wanted to feel real gravity and breathe real air. We used to talk about it all the time. How it would feel to hold the dirt of a living world in our hands. How the grass would feel under our feet." She paused and wiped her eyes. "Now she'll be part of that dirt, part of that grass." Aunt Marci looked up from Bethany's still body. "Thank you all for trying so hard, and risking your lives so that she could be here."

My head pounded. No one had accused me of causing her death. No one mentioned a thing about it. But Nirah knew. She had supervised the loading and tie-down of all the gear we were bringing back from Horizon. She knew I had loosened the nets and not clamped them back down. And we both knew that crate would never have jarred loose at our landing if I hadn't pulled those ropes off.

I looked down into Bethany's open grave. Covered with the fabric, she looked just like Erik had, lying in the hole I had helped dig for him.

Words were echoing around my head. "Fly free, Bethany." Everyone was saying it, clustered around the hole in the ground. They were standing right on top of Erik's grave where we hadn't even put up a marker yet.

"Josh? Josh, what are you doing? Stop it." I heard people saying my name, but there was nothing in my vision but the dark hole. People were grabbing at my arms and there was something warm running down my face. I held up my palms. Red, all caked under my fingernails. My vision blurred, and the world turned yellow. I was dimly aware that I was screaming before everything went black.

CHAPTER 37

CALEB

We rumbled back to the mountains with a day to spare. Since the satellite still seemed to be down, we hadn't heard a word from anyone. We didn't know if the shuttle had survived the launch, or docked successfully with Horizon. But when we broke through the trees into the clearing, there it was. It appeared to have been a rough landing, and a huge skid of broken ground made a trail behind its final resting place. It hadn't been smooth, but the shuttle had survived. I was going to see my dad again.

Before the tank even stopped I had thrown open the top and jumped off. I raced up the rocky incline to the tunnel that led to the Painted Hall.

Staci met me in the narrow tunnel. She barred my way past and grabbed my shoulders. "Caleb, stop, you have to wait."

But I couldn't wait. "Where's my dad? Is everyone okay?" I pushed past her and ran down the corridor.

Just inside the giant hall I ran into Mayor Borin.

"Where's my dad?"

He looked at me with sad eyes, but I was too excited to pay attention. "Caleb, come on into the briefing room."

I assumed that's where my dad would be, getting up to speed on how things worked around Carthage. Of course he'd be on the council. Maybe he'd even take my seat, which was fine with me. Governing was for other people.

There was no one in the briefing room.

"Caleb, your mom is with Josh in the infirmary. She's got him sedated for now."

My mouth went dry. "Josh? What happened? Is he all right?"

Mayor Borin told me. It was as if the Horizon Alpha had crashed straight into me, crushing me from space into a flat, dead pile of nothing.

Staci came into the room and put her arms around me, and I sobbed into her shoulder.

Dad wasn't coming home. And Josh might never recover from that.

I stumbled out of the room and through the hall, numb to the condolences from the people moving around me. In the tiny infirmary ward I found Mom sitting on the edge of the bed where Josh was sleeping. She jumped up and ran to me, and we cried together for what felt like hours.

"Your father said to tell you how proud he was of you," she murmured into my shoulder. "He saved everyone on the shuttle."

I pulled away and looked at my brother. His face was all bandaged up. "It's too soon. He only went up there to save Dad because he couldn't handle Erik dying. Poor Josh."

Mom sat back onto his bed. The movement did not wake him. "And there was an accident during the landing. Don's daughter didn't make it."

Bethany. *Oh, no. Poor Don.* All the nasty things I'd thought about him melted away. *Poor Don.*

"Josh had . . . an episode at her funeral." Mom's hand brushed the bandages over Josh's eyes. "It was too soon after losing Erik. He was ripping at his own skin, almost took out his eye. I've kept him sedated for a couple of days. He just needs to rest."

As always, there was no time to mourn the lost. "But they got everyone else down, right? And all the stuff we need?" I hated asking about the stupid equipment, but sometime in the next forty-eight hours, the Flood would arrive. As I had done so many times in the 'saur-filled jungle, I pushed my grief away for the moment. "Are we ready?"

Mom nodded. "They've been working nonstop for days, climbing around the mountains and testing the system. If it's volume that keeps those little monsters away, we should be just fine."

Josh stirred and his lips opened for a moment before closing again.

"Can he hear me?"

"Maybe. He probably won't remember when he wakes up."

I knelt next to the bed and whispered into his ear. "Josh? Hey, buddy, it's me, Caleb. Just wanted to say I'm so glad you're my brother. You did it. You saved those people and got us the stuff we need to save everyone here. So just . . ." I sniffled into my sleeve. "Just hang in there. I'm gonna get us through these next few days and then . . . then we'll figure it out. We always do."

He didn't answer and didn't move.

I gave Mom one more hug and trudged out of the infirmary toward the valley. It wasn't yet real to me that Dad wasn't coming home. That we'd found him only to lose him again when we were so close. It would hit me soon enough. But if Nirah and Sara were right, the Flood could be here as early as tonight. And if we weren't ready, we could lose everyone.

CHAPTER 38

SHIRO

All the able climbers had pitched in to run wire and place the speakers. After a few hours' sleep in my own little cavern, so welcome after the sweaty confines of the tank, I joined the crew hoisting the last speaker into place at the northwest edge of the ring of mountains around our valley. We didn't have enough wire to power each one independently, so they were on a huge circuit going all the way around the valley. Each speaker depended on power flowing from the one ahead of it in line. Nobody liked that, but there was nothing else we could do. Fernando and I were on top, with Carmen feeding us wire from just below.

I would have preferred to be up here with Caleb. Carmen was stronger than she looked, but I was none too pleased to have her clinging onto the rocks behind me. Caleb was a mess about the loss of his dad, though, and had been up all night climbing up and down like a madman, frantic to get the wires run. He was dead on his feet and didn't even argue when I pulled the coil of wire from his hands and shoved him toward the caves. When

Carmen stepped up to take his place, I wanted to say no, but she had as much to lose as anyone else, and as much right to be up here as any of the guys.

Just over the edge was a steep drop leading to a wide open plain with a clear lake on the far side where the rocky hills picked up again. Caleb and his gang had gone around it on their way to rescue the Transport Eight crew because there were always 'saurs there, usually some sort of Brachi or one of the other plant-eaters. But where there was prey, there were always hunters.

No 'saurs browsed the trees at the edge of the hills today. That should have made me feel safer, exposed at the top of the mountain, but instead it chilled me in the cool height.

They're avoiding this whole area right now. They know what's coming.

"Here, hold this." Fernando handed me the coil of wire.

I patched the wire into the back of the speaker. "Is this it? Are we ready?"

Fernando shrugged. "Our part's done. If they really do come through here. If this noise thing works at all."

Carmen spoke up from below us. "If they come and this doesn't work, we'll know soon enough. And for a very short time." Her words sounded cavalier, but the tremor in her voice wasn't just from the height.

I looked over the edge, out onto the empty field. Movement at the base of the sheer cliff caught my eye. A couple of small creatures had emerged from the tall grass and were scaling the rocks. They headed straight for Fernando and me.

"Hey, look at those." I pointed down the rocks. "What are they?"

Fernando peered over. "No idea. Quick, though."

We both had pistols, and new lightning sticks made from the stuff brought down from Horizon. Some of the smaller, rock-hopper 'saurs got curious when we were up here, and a quick jolt from the lightning stick would send them on their way.

The three little creatures continued their beeline climb. As they got closer, I could see how fast they were, with four legs gripping the wall in sharp little talons. They had short, stubby tails, and large, pointy heads. The whole 'saur looked about the size of my boot. We'd been digging up rotted bodies with heads just like this for weeks.

Oh, no. We're not ready.

The first one reached the top of the cliff and jumped straight at Fernando. He wielded his lightning stick like a baseball bat, sending the little 'saur flying out over the edge.

"Why'd you do that? Sara would have loved for us to catch it." I knelt down to see the other two close behind.

Fernando snorted. "We don't need any more pet 'saurs."

These would never be pets.

From below us on the Carthage side, Carmen called up to us. "Are we done here? Time to go down?"

"In a second," I said. "Going to try and get one of these things."

The first of the two reached the top and jumped at Fernando. He swung his stick at it but missed, and the little beast shot up his leg, gripping with the sharp claws. It buried its face in his armpit and Fernando shrieked, whacking at it with the butt of his lightning stick.

"Get it off! Get it off me!" I grabbed at it and got hold of its back legs. When I pulled it free, it took a large chunk of Fernando's flesh with it. Without thinking, I flung it over the sheer edge.

Fernando collapsed, clutching his armpit. Blood stained his shirt and seeped through his fingers.

"Stars, that thing was trying to eat you."

The third one crested the hill, and I zapped it with my lightning stick as it skittered toward me. It fell to the ground, twitching, but in a second was staggering to its feet. I hit it with the zapper again. After three more electric jolts, it finally stopped moving.

"Carmen, get up here," I called to her. "Something's bit Fernando."

She was already scrambling up the hill toward her bleeding brother. We pulled his shirt off to reveal at least seven bloody bites, each one a deep, open gash where the creature's teeth had carved right through his skin.

"Is this what I think it is?" The chill I'd felt looking over the empty valley returned. *You know what it is. You saw this same sharp head rotting on a pile of its own eggs.*

Carmen saw the dead 'saur at my feet.

"It's here. They're coming. We have to get down right now. Right now." She babbled through trembling lips.

I grabbed her hand before she could bolt away down the hillside. "Carmen, we need you. You have to help me get Fernando down. But is this for sure one of them? The Flood 'saurs?"

She nodded, never taking her eyes off the little body, its mouth still bloody. "There's always a couple that come right before the rest. They trickle in for the first few hours. Then the rest come." She looked at me with horror in her face. "Then we all die."

CHAPTER 39

CALEB

We kept watch all night.

After Carmen and Shiro got Fernando down from the mountain and into the infirmary, we gave the dead Flood 'saur to Sara.

"It's a male." She turned the little body over in her hands. "Look at the jaw. Just like the dead females we dug up. It's like a piranha. Look at the teeth." Her voice was clipped and high, the way it got when she was afraid. "Hundreds of thousands of these are coming."

Everything was ready. Horizon's speakers faced out of every low pass. We had brought Ryenne's little 'saurs into the lowest room of the cave system and padded the room with cut grass, fabric, and everything else we could find to dampen the sound. They were jumpy when we brought them in from the field, darting around and looking up at the mountains around the valley. They weren't going to like the next few days, but there was nothing more we could do. Our sheep were locked in their shed with plenty of water and food to last the next few days.

The council had deliberated about sending the youngest children and babies out with their mothers into the shuttle. If our plan didn't work, the only safe place might be locked inside it. But if our plan did work, it would be safer in the valley, and we might not be able to get to them to bring them back inside until the torrent of tiny 'saurs passed us by, which the Birdmens' painting seemed to indicate might take at least three days. Since Mom was one of those whose fate was being discussed, she had gotten her say.

"I'm not hiding in a shuttle. If this doesn't work, I don't want to be the only one left. We stand or fall together."

In the end, we came up with a compromise. We ringed the wide rock plateau that was the entrance to our cave system with firewood and stacked plenty inside the ring. The children and babies, along with anyone who couldn't climb and help with the lookout, camped inside. If those of us on the outside failed and the Flood came in, we hoped the ring of fire would keep them safe.

The look on Mayor Borin's face was almost worth the risk. Since he was confined to a wheelchair and the only exit into the valley was down a steep flight of stairs, he hadn't left the caves since we arrived. He'd never seen our valley, and when we carried him down the stairs and brought him out into the evening twilight, he was near tears with joy.

He clutched my arm as we set him into his chair. "It's amazing. This place . . . it's so beautiful. I had no idea anything could be this beautiful." I helped him maneuver his chair over to the cleared fire ring and got him settled for the night before heading inside to sleep for a few hours before my watch.

I woke long before dawn and plodded downstairs to the plateau. Shiro and I were assigned to lookout stations at the northwest rim of the valley. I hugged Mom and Malia one last time, and joined the group of men and women heading out to relieve those who had been on patrol all day. They were watching the pine forest for any new hatches that were missed in the Flood egg hunt, and for more stragglers coming over the mountains.

Nirah had adjusted the oxygen delivery on our welding torches to turn them into flamethrowers. All day long we had seen intermittent blasts at the edges of the rocky hills as our people blasted the Flood 'saurs coming in by twos and threes. But I had just seen what one of those little monsters did to Fernando. If the noise didn't work and we were overrun, even a flamethrower wouldn't help.

Shiro and I headed out with the rest of the group. On the way across the valley, we passed the little graveyard. A lone figure knelt at the newest grave. Don had held a solitary vigil since we returned in our tank, neither eating nor sleeping. There was nothing any of us could say. We had all lost so many that we loved. Every person in Carthage knew the pain.

At the bottom of the hill, Shiro and I parted ways, climbing up to our individual lookout points. Our positions were close enough to see each other, but not close enough to have an easy conversation. I sat alone with my thoughts in the moonlight.

Our sat trans had no connection since Horizon went down. *With Dad on it.* I pushed that thought from my mind, and turned the trans over in my hands. Mayor Borin had spent the past couple of days rigging up a crude transistor, so a few of our sat trans now worked as two way radios. There was no chatter on the radio. Only tense silence.

A cool wind kicked up dust and I rubbed grit out of my eyes. I glanced back down across the valley. The protective ring plateau wasn't lit, but smaller campfires still burned inside the ring. I was too far to hear any noise from inside, but I was certain that no one down there was sleeping.

The full moon sank lower in the sky. Dawn was just breaking, the first pink blush lightening the sky over the empty hills. It cast a dark, moving shadow over the mountain in the distance.

My eyes adjusted to the brightening landscape.

The shadow moved.

Oh, scat. Here they come.

I fumbled with the sat trans, keying in the "talk" code, unable to tear my eyes off the horrific sight before me. "They're coming! Lookout Station Four, Caleb Wilde, they're coming!"

It looked like the mountain was alive. There had to be a million of them. They flowed like a waterfall over the mountain, splitting off into smaller rivers and joining back up into a massive tide of dark undulation. They truly were a flood.

The air above them was full of fliers. I pressed myself into the rocks at my back as two small pterosaurs skimmed over my head, aimed for the rolling wave of 'saurs.

One by one, they dove into the moving carpet and plucked out individuals, grasped in their talons. They didn't all make it. As I watched, a large brown flier lingered too close, grabbing for a hopping Flood 'saur. Dozens of them leaped onto the flier's wings and pulled it down into the crowd. I was too far to hear if it screamed, but it didn't emerge from the torrent.

"Get everyone into the caves!" I yelled into the radio. "There's fliers everywhere!" Our people would be easy pickings for the cloud of pterosaurs that circled around the approaching Flood.

I jammed my earplugs in tight. Any second now the speakers at my feet would blare out their noise. Then we would see if humans would live another day on Tau Ceti e.

The Flood poured off the mountain. *Will they ever stop coming?* The smallest trickle in the lead was tumbling toward the base of our hill. There were thousands. Millions. More every second.

Come on, come on. Where's the noise? What were they doing?

Dawn lit the open plain where the Flood poured across.

We're dead. We're all dead. Why is there no noise?

The speakers should be working by now. I tore my eyes from the oncoming hoard, and crouched down to check the wires on my speaker. Everything seemed tight but there was still no sound. I punched the code and yelled into the radio again, and called across the hilltop to Shiro.

"Why aren't the speakers working?"

I could barely hear his "I don't know!" response, but all around the circle of mountains that ringed our valley, the lookouts took up the call. "Check your wires! They're here!"

CHAPTER 40

JOSH

I was already awake when the pandemonium started. The sedatives Mom had given me wore off, leaving me with a splitting headache and a mouth that tasted like Brachi scat. When I emerged into the Painted Hall, people were running for the staircase.

"What's happened? Are they here?"

The small crowd swept me up, with more tired-looking people joining us in the corridor.

"Speakers aren't working. Everybody grab a flamethrower."

We pounded down the staircase and out into the early dawn light. Mayor Borin and Nirah were outside near the empty fire ring, red shadows dancing on the rocks. They both swore at the amplifier from which wires ran out in each direction.

"Why isn't it working? It worked last night when we tested it." Nirah pried the back off the amplifier and shone a light inside.

"I don't know." Mayor Borin cast a worried look out onto the hilltops. "But they're coming. If we can't get this working in the next few minutes . . ." He didn't need to finish. Everyone knew.

A call came across the radio. "Get everyone into the caves, there's fliers everywhere!"

We all looked to the sky. Nothing yet. But whoever made that call would be higher up, facing out of the valley.

The mothers with babies jumped up, clutching their little ones to their chests.

"Get in, get inside!" I grabbed two toddlers that were hanging on their mother's legs and followed her in and up the staircase, holding the screaming children. When we got to the top, I set them down. "Run inside, guys, Follow your mom." They dashed away down the dim hallway.

When the flood of women and children was past, I ran back down the staircase. Erik's voice chuckled in my head. *Careful, there. Watch your step.* I swallowed the lump in my throat and pounded down to the plateau.

Nirah was arguing with Mayor Borin.

"You've got to get inside. I can handle this, but I can't carry you if those fliers come."

Mayor Borin grunted. "Death from the air, death on the ground, all the same to me. I'll go inside when we get this scatting speaker on."

Nirah turned a look on me that clearly said, "Talk some sense into him." But it was his decision, not mine, and not Nirah's.

"I'm heading out to . . ." I trailed off. I had no idea what I was going to do out there. But Mayor Borin was right. Whatever direction it came from, if tonight was my night, I was going to face it under the open sky. "I'm going out to help," I said.

All the flamethrowers were gone by the time I got to the crate of weapons. I fished around at the bottom and found a flare gun.

A flare gun. Against a hundred thousand hungry 'saurs.

The memory of Erik snorted in my head. *You've faced some long odds, but I think this might be it. Take a few with you on your way out. See you soon, buddy.*

The thought brought a little smile to my lips. Erik had hated 'saurs more than anyone else on this hot, heavy planet. If we were all going to die today, eaten by a million little mouths, maybe it was better that he wasn't here to see it. A quick fall to the bottom of a staircase was no doubt easier than the fate that awaited every human left on Tau Ceti e.

I tucked the flare gun into the back of my pants, and headed out across the field.

CHAPTER 41

CALEB

The bulk of the Flood hadn't reached us yet. They were halfway across the wide plain, heading straight for us. But the grass ahead of them was alive with the fastest of the group, a hundred 'saurs broken away from the pack and leading the charge.

"Northwest quadrant, get back from the edge!" I shouted into my radio. "Don't let them see you or they'll climb straight up!"

I ducked back behind a large boulder, tearing my eyes from the oncoming wave of death. Maybe if they didn't see us on top of the cliff, they wouldn't bother making the climb. Maybe they'd go around.

Rocks fell over the inside edge as I crouched down, peering over.

Down the hill in the valley, the first of the Flood 'saurs came pouring out a tiny hole between the rocks.

They were getting inside.

I waved my flamethrower in the air to get Shiro's attention. The little line of 'saurs was almost directly beneath him. He saw me and I gestured down the mountain. We made eye contact across the pass, threw our flamethrowers over our backs, and scrambled off the mountaintop.

Shiro got to the bottom first. He blasted his flamethrower in an arc around him, but the 'saurs kept coming, running right over the charred bodies of their brethren.

My foot slipped and I slid down the last five meters. The flamethrower bounced off my shoulder and I lunged to retrieve it.

By the time I got to Shiro, he was overwhelmed. Tiny 'saurs were crawling up his legs and jumping onto his neck.

What do I do? If I turned the flamethrower on him, I'd burn him right along with the 'saurs.

He dropped his flamethrower and rolled on the ground. I shot an arc of flame all around him, but they were still pouring through the hole.

Stop them coming in or they'll get us all.

I had to ignore Shiro's screams. The 'saurs were coming through a hole in the rock, a tiny tunnel we would never have noticed. I stuck the end of my flamethrower straight into the hole, flinging away the 'saurs that jumped right onto my arms. Shreds of my shirt and bloody skin splattered away with them.

With bloody hands, I hit the trigger. Fire poured into the tunnel. The smell of burning 'saur wafted out.

That won't hold them for long.

But I had done this before.

I ran around Shiro, blasting every Flood 'saur I could see. A few had surely made it past, heading for our people, but hopefully not enough to do much damage. There were others with flamethrowers stationed around the orchards and fields. Hopefully they'd clean up these few.

One more blast in the tunnel with the flamethrower bought me a few more seconds. I had no doubt that the 'saurs would push right through the burned ones to come through, and fast.

I flung myself down next to Shiro and pulled the 'saurs off him. He was still moving, but no longer screaming. *Not a good sign.* His clothes were in tatters and blood seeped through every ragged hole.

And there was still silence from the speakers on top of the cliffs.

Stop them. Close the hole. The rest will be here in minutes.

Shiro was dead weight as I grabbed him under the armpits to drag him away. No new 'saurs were coming through the hole, but it wouldn't be long. And Shiro was heavy.

Adam ran over to us and picked up Shiro's legs. Together we carried him into the copse of trees at this end of the valley.

I set Shiro down, and grabbed the radio from his belt. "Get him back to the cave! They're getting through!" Adam opened his mouth to argue, but I shooed him away and ran back toward the hole, pausing to grab a long stick from the ground.

'Saurs were pouring out again, flopping to the ground and running straight toward me. I opened fire with my flamethrower, roasting anything that moved. One more time I stuck the nozzle into the tunnel and blasted.

I lowered the flamethrower and scrambled for my belt.

The haul from Horizon was more than just speakers.

I ripped a grenade from my belt and pulled the pin. It fit straight into the hole and I shoved it as deep as I could with the stick before dropping it and sprinting away.

The blast knocked me off my feet.

I lay there dazed for a moment. Rolling onto my back, I looked toward the hole.

A pile of rubble was all that was left of that little section of mountainside. Nothing came through.

The smell of blood hit my nostrils and I remembered that the dark smears on my clothes were not just Shiro's. Little chunks of flesh were missing all over my arms and legs. I was far too hyped up to feel pain at that moment, but I looked like something out of a zombie film.

The pain hit when I tried to stand up. Dizziness washed over me as the adrenaline pumped out of my system. I sank back down to the ground and pawed at my belt for Shiro's radio, gasping out my message.

"Get everyone down! They're coming through the cracks. Flamethrowers and grenades!"

Strong hands gripped around my chest and lifted me up. I staggered into Josh, who caught me before I fell again. His face was covered in dry scabs. He looked like a horror movie, but I was never so glad to see anyone in my life.

"Caleb, are you okay?"

I nodded. "What's wrong with the speakers? They're here. They're going to get in everywhere."

He shook his head. "Nirah and Borin don't know. They're working on it.

My radio crackled to life. "Everyone, check your wires. There's nothing wrong at our end. We must have lost the circuit. Find the break!"

There were kilometers of wire strung all around the valley. *How are we going to find one broken speaker?*

I leaned on Josh and we emerged from the trees into the morning sunlight. Our people were scrambling over the rocks here and there, looking for the broken wire. *Not enough. We'll never find it.*

"There! That's gotta be it!" Josh pointed up the north wall and I followed his gaze.

A pterosaur was sitting at the top edge of the cliff, peering down into the valley.

It was sitting right on one of our speakers.

CHAPTER 42

SHIRO

A thunderous crash woke me up and I bolted upright. Every inch of my skin was screaming.

"Hold on, Shiro." Adam's face came into fuzzy focus. "We need to get you back to the cave, but nobody can help us. Can you walk?"

I can barely breathe.

"Yeah, I'm okay," I said. "Just . . . help me up." There was no confusion in my mind. I remembered every second until I blacked out with a hundred little 'saurs eating me alive. Adam had pulled off my shirt and ripped it into strips, tying them around my arms and legs. Blood seeped through them all, making me look like a horror movie mummy risen from the dead. Which was pretty much what I felt like. "Why aren't the speakers working?"

"I don't know." Adam cast a worried glance at the hillside behind us. "Caleb and Josh just went busting up there to fix something, but I don't know what's wrong." He pulled out his canteen and offered it to me. The water was cold and sweet and I felt life flowing back into me as I swallowed.

He helped me to my feet and I leaned on him for a moment as the world spun around me. A few more sips of water and it slowed enough for me to shuffle one foot in front of the other, a bloody arm draped around Adam for support.

"You're doing great," Adam said. "Slow and steady."

We plodded through the pine trees and around the east side of the lake. Adrenaline was kicking in with each step, the pain dulling to a muted throb. I always walked with a slight limp, ever since my leg was broken, but this morning I barely noticed that old familiar pain under this bright, new one all over me. My face itched and I raised a bloody hand to touch it, but Adam batted it away.

"Don't touch it. You'll get yourself bleeding again."

A scream cut through the morning air.

Carmen.

I'd know her voice anywhere.

I stopped, head snapping from side to side. Where had it come from?

She screamed again.

"There!" I pulled away from Adam and shuffled toward the sound. Faster. Help her.

"You can't help anybody," Adam said, grabbing at my shoulder, but I pushed him aside and jogged across the field in the shadow of the mountain.

Gunshots. A lot of them.

Carmen was standing with her back to us, firing a semiautomatic rifle they must have brought down from Horizon. Her shots were wild as the heavy weapon bucked in her hands. Bullets pinged off the rocks on the hillside.

And a trail of Flood 'saurs poured down from the low point in the wall.

I had no weapons. No flamethrower, no grenades. All I could do was look on as Adam rushed up behind her and grabbed the rifle from her hands. He mowed down the little 'saurs in their line, but more flowed over to take their place.

"There's a million of them!" The call came down from above where Carmen and Adam were shooting. I squinted up into the light to where Fernando was looking over the far edge. "They're coming through here!"

My exhaustion and pain fell away. While Adam fired away at the steady stream of 'saurs heading right toward him, I bolted up the hill toward Fernando. The slope was shallow and I reached him on the edge of a large basin between the inner and outer ridges of our protective wall. Without even looking at me, he pointed over the edge.

It was teeming with Flood 'saurs.

They were climbing over the far wall and falling into the basin. There was only one small place for them to climb up the inner wall, but there were enough in there to kill every man, woman, and child in the Carthage caves. We had to stop them.

Fernando had two grenades on his belt. He knocked my hand away when I reached for one.

"Already tried," he said. "They're all spread out down there. Killed a bunch, but a bunch more came right over."

I peered over to the far wall. There was a ton of rock on the cliff above the low spot where the 'saurs were coming in. If we could get it to fall, it might plug the hole.

Fernando followed my gaze. "Tried that, too. Grenade's not enough."

A gentle hand touched my shoulder, and Don Rand stood behind me, a shoulder-held rocket launcher in his arms.

"Move aside. I've got this."

"Where did you get that?"

He gave a grim smile. "Came down from Horizon. Bethany's gift to the 'saurs."

Fernando and I backed away and Don knelt on the sloping ground. He aimed the launcher straight at the rocks above the low pass on the far wall. There was a huge bang, followed by a distant explosion that vibrated right through my boots. The wall above the hole crumbled, huge boulders sliding down. Most of them blew over the far side of the wall, but enough fell into the gap that the rush of 'saurs stopped coming.

My ears rang. Over the tinny buzz, I heard Fernando say, "That should buy us a little time on that side."

But they were still pouring out of the basin and into our valley.

"Do you have another round for that thing?" I shouted at Don. If my ears were ringing, his must be almost useless.

He laid the rocket launcher down, clearly not hearing me. But it answered my question. If he could fire it again, he'd have aimed it down at the writhing pool of 'saurs below us. He motioned toward the grenades on Fernando's belt.

I mimed that they were too spread out for a grenade to work.

A sad smile came over Don's features. He looked down the steep slope to where the 'saurs were all scrambling to get up and over into our valley. Quicker than I would have thought possible, he grabbed the grenades from Fernando's belt and slid away from us down the hill.

He caught himself on a rock just a meter above the roiling pile of 'saurs. They smelled his warm odor and swarmed underneath him, coming from all sides of the basin to jump up toward the rock he stood on.

"No!" I yelled, but he was past hearing me.

He pulled the pins on the grenades, one by one.

He stepped over the edge into the sea of hungry teeth.

I turned away before the blasts that killed them all.

CHAPTER 43

CALEB

Josh and I looked up the hill to where the flier perched on our speaker. We bolted for the rocks. Josh pulled a flare gun from the back of his pants and tossed it to me as we ran. "You're hurt. I'll get up faster. Cover me."

I still had the flamethrower on my back, weighing me down, and added the flare gun to the pistol in my pocket. Josh scrambled up the mountain well ahead of me.

When he got near the pterosaur, he started yelling and waving the free arm that wasn't clutched onto the rock.

It wasn't a huge one. It wouldn't be able to carry off a full-grown human. That didn't make it any less deadly. It hissed at Josh, who kept climbing toward it, yelling like a banshee, grabbing rocks and hurling them at the beast on our speaker.

One of the rocks hit it square in the jaw. With a final hiss, it opened its wings and pushed off, sailing over our heads.

The force of its push sent the speaker it had been sitting on crashing over the far side of the cliff.

"The speaker! Get the speaker back!"

Josh heard me and scampered up the last of the climb. By the time I made it to the top, he was already over the edge.

I dropped to my knees and peered over. The speaker had broken off one wire, which was thankfully still anchored on the rocks at my right hand. It was still attached to the other, five meters down, sitting on a ledge and teetering over the edge.

From here, I could see the upper edge of the plain. The full force of the Flood was almost here. A rattling sound of gunfire echoed out of the valley, but I couldn't take my eyes away from my brother.

"Be careful," I called down to Josh. "But . . . hurry."

Josh reached the speaker and stood with his toes on the ledge. He looked up at me. It was too far to hand it up. The speaker was small, only about six inches in diameter, and he tucked it inside his shirt with the wire trailing out. "I'm coming up! Be ready!"

The wave of the Flood had reached the bottom of the cliff.

Hurry, hurry, hurry.

More gunfire popped through the valley. A raspy scream broke the air above us and the pterosaur zoomed in straight over my head. It banked hard in the air and dove straight for Josh, hanging on the wall.

"Get down!" I yelled, and he pressed himself low against the rocks as the pterosaur's claws scrambled at the rocks where his head had just been.

I pulled out the pistol and fired at the beast as it shoved away from the wall and circled around for another run. If I hit it, the bullet didn't slow it down. It dove for Josh again.

He was five feet below me.

I fired at the pterosaur, coming straight in toward us.

Click.

It wasn't the sound Wolves made in their throats, but the noise of an empty pistol. Meant the same thing, though. Death was coming.

I dropped it at my feet and pawed into my pocket. *Where is it? Where is it?*

Josh's eyes were wide as he launched up toward me. I lunged over his head and shot a flare straight into the open mouth of the pterosaur. Its head jerked back, jaws snapping inches from Josh's leg.

He threw himself up over the ledge and pulled the speaker out of his shirt. "Please work, please work, please work."

The Flood was more than halfway up the wall of the cliff. They would be here in seconds.

A huge boom rattled through the hills.

"Wire it up! Plug it in!" I screamed.

The injured pterosaur flapped crazily at the edge of the cliff, wind buffeting my face.

I whipped the flamethrower from my back and roasted the flier right out of the sky. It bounced down the cliff front, knocking off hundreds of Flood 'saurs as it fell.

"I got it!" Josh yelled. "This is it!"

Every speaker roared to life.

The screech made me drop my radio, which tumbled down the rocks toward the swarming 'saurs below.

I gripped the flamethrower, peering over at the Flood beneath me.

The tiny 'saurs were a roaring tide, but now they were trying to flow backwards. Those in the lead, who had been almost to the top of our hillside, were pouring back down into the throng. They crashed like a wave onto those at the bottom of the hill where they split into two turbulent rivers, flowing around our little valley to each side.

I raised my flamethrower and gave two short blasts. All around the circle, the blasts were repeated. It was working. The plan was actually working. Like the Birdmen before us, the humans of Carthage Valley were holding off the Flood.

Josh was collapsed on the rocks at my feet. The noise from the speakers pounded into my skull, and his head was right next to it. His face was scabbed and crusted, and his hands bloody when he reached up and grabbed my arms, staring straight into my eyes.

He mouthed the words clearly.

I'm glad you're my brother.

CHAPTER 44

CAPTAIN THEODORE WILDE

I don't know if Josh heard my final call or not. There was no way to release that arm from inside their shuttle. I had to stay behind. My comm system went out as the shuttle peeled away from Horizon, and I watched his face for just a moment, pressed against the thick glass as they flew away. It's the expression that will haunt me until I die.

Which won't be very long now.

I was captain of the great ark Horizon Alpha for eleven years before we reached Tau Ceti e, and never could figure out why there were escape pods on the outer ring of Tube One. Over the long days before they finally heard our call on the planet's surface, we stocked one of the pods with water and food. There was no way rescue was coming, and we didn't want to burn up with Horizon when she finally crashed into the planet below. We didn't honestly think we'd survive the fall. It had a huge parachute that would open automatically after entry into the atmosphere, and rockets that were supposed to fire when we neared the surface, which probably wouldn't work after all this time. And even if they did, they wouldn't be powerful enough to stop us from a very hard landing.

But there was a tiny chance.

If we got extraordinarily lucky, at least some of us might possibly live long enough to pop the hatch. Breathe the air of a living planet. The pod had no guidance, so there was absolutely no chance we'd land close enough for anyone to rescue us, even if we did survive. We all agreed it was worth the chance, since we were all going to die anyway.

Darned if they didn't come and get us on Horizon, though.

Everyone got safely aboard the shuttle, and when it became obvious that the arm wasn't letting go, there was no decision. In the oldest maritime tradition, the captain would go down with his ship.

I watched my son beat his head against the window as the shuttle broke away. My feet were hanging in space, and I gripped the manual arm-release handle to keep from sailing out the open hatch into black, empty space.

"I'm going to try to get to the pod!" I called, but realized my comm had gone dead. Better that way, really. I'd hate for anyone to think they might come and find me.

Horizon's self-destruct was already set to blow the ship into pieces for entry. She was heading toward the atmosphere where she would break apart and burn up. The parts that made it through would crash into the opposite side of the planet from my family's valley home.

I knew where each of the charges would blow up. I could have sat on one, been instantly and painlessly vaporized when Horizon exploded.

But there was fresh air down there. With the taste of fresh fruit still on my lips, I couldn't ignore the call.

Time, time, time. We had so much of it in three years up here, and it came down to ten minutes. Probably nine.

The pod was on the opposite side of Tube One, stilled in its rotation years ago. My arms ached from pushing off wall after wall as I careened through the ship, launching myself down the dark corridors. The headlamp on my suit helmet still worked, and cut a shimmering path through the hazy vacuum.

Five minutes. Maybe four.

The pod door was open. I shoved myself through it and bolted the hatch behind me. No time to strap in.

A screaming tug on the release lever triggered a small thrust that pushed the pod away from Horizon toward the glow of the planet below.

I pushed myself into a seat and pulled the safety harness across my lap.

One minute.

If I was too close when Horizon blew, this would be a very short escape.

A soundless explosion lit the dark window and the pod bucked under me, spinning toward the atmosphere. Out the tiny porthole window, I could see the flashes—one, two, three—of Horizon's self-destruct. Then the darkness was filled with fire. Gravity from the planet tightened its grip on my pod and I fell out of the sky in a burning blaze.

With a bone-jarring jolt, the pod lurched and righted itself.

Parachute opened.

But I was falling way too fast.

I couldn't see what I was heading for, but my stomach told me I was plummeting out of the sky.

Come on, thrusters.

They worked.

But they weren't enough.

The crash came sooner than I expected, and knocked me out cold.

I woke up in pain everywhere. The pod was rocking slightly.

Somehow, I was alive.

The hatch was sitting at an angle above my head. My seat

harness had broken at impact, and I pulled myself up to the latch.

Fresh air. I was going to smell fresh air.

It took all I had to pop the hatch. I pulled off my helmet and dropped it to the floor of the pod with a crunch.

The smell was worth every moment of pain. I breathed it in, a tangy, salty odor, so rich and clean. It revived me enough to climb up on the seat and stick my head out.

It was evening. A huge red sun was setting over a flat, distant horizon. The land under the pod was moving, and it took my addled brain a moment to realize it wasn't land at all, but water.

My pod had crash landed in the ocean.

It rocked under my feet and I turned to look the other way. I was washed up on the beach of a small island.

There might be dinosaurs here, but it hardly mattered. I was on the opposite side of the planet from anyone who knew I was alive. The pod had an emergency beacon, but with no satellites to pick it up, no one would ever hear it.

Didn't matter. I knew I was dead when the shuttle left without me.

But I was going to feel that sand.

I peeled off my suit, wincing with every movement. Moving was easier without it, and I hauled myself out of the hatch, sliding down the outside of the pod and landing with a splash in the shallow water lapping at the golden sand beach.

Real land. A real planet.

And I got at least some of our people here safely.

I lay in the last of the sunlight, feeling warm water flowing around my body, cradled in soft sand.

My sons and daughter would survive. Their sons and daughters would survive. This terrible, glorious, living planet would provide for the children of Horizon Alpha.

CHAPTER 45

CALEB

Somehow Josh and I got down the mountain and back to the cave. I was still hopped up on adrenaline and feeling no pain when one of the medics cleaned my wounds and wrapped up my arms and legs. After an hour's rest, my skin started to throb. *Get up. Get out here and forget about it.* I grabbed a few bites of fruit and refilled my canteen before heading back out into the valley where every able-bodied person patrolled the inner walls with flamethrowers, blasting away at the few 'saurs that had scrambled through cracks in the mountain. My hearing was muffled and Josh was almost deaf, but Mom thought it was probably temporary.

No one slept for three days. Our speakers screamed out day and night until late on the third afternoon when I climbed the mountain to see the last wave flow around the edge of the field.

As suddenly as they had arrived, the final stragglers skittered around our valley. When the speakers were finally turned off, the silence pounded into our skulls just like the noise had.

It was touch and go with Shiro for the first forty-eight hours.

He'd collapsed from blood loss at the bottom of the slope where Don brought the hillside down to buy our valley the moments we needed to wire our speaker. Mom said that without the blood transfusion supplies that the mission to Horizon brought down, there would have been no chance for Shiro to recover. As it was, he looked like he'd been through a meat grinder, with chunks of flesh missing pretty much all over him. He would be in bandages for weeks.

I wasn't in great shape myself, but I was a darned sight better than him. The nasty little Flood 'saurs had chewed up my arms and legs, and every time the bandages were pulled off I had to bite on a thick strip of 'saur hide since I wasn't taking any of our very limited supply of painkillers. Sara was working on distilling some kind of narcotic from the thorns of the bush that almost killed me, but nothing was ready yet, so I bit down and didn't look as my wounds were dressed and re-wrapped.

The morning after the Flood ended, Shiro was awake, but groggy. After another two days of my mother's watchful care, he was chafing in the cool infirmary, so Josh and I each got under a shoulder and helped him out onto the plateau.

He turned his bandaged face to the bright sun. "That's what I need. Time and sunshine."

We had moved Ryenne's 'saurs back out into their pen. They had fussed and chirped the entire time they were confined during the Flood, but Ryenne managed to make them a reasonably quiet hideaway in the depths of the caves. The two little 'saurs were as happy as Shiro to see the sun again when it was all over.

Nirah said in a couple of weeks, the pregnant Flood 'saurs would come waddling back through the mountains toward wherever they laid their eggs in the far north. Everyone was looking forward to a little payback.

"I think your mom counted a hundred and twelve bites," Shiro said, picking at the bandage on his left arm. "So I plan to kill a hundred and twelve of the little jerks when they come back through. We should make it a holiday. Call it the 'Feast of Retaliation.'"

I wasn't sure Shiro would be up to a mass 'saur slaughter in a few weeks' time, even if they were slow and fat and not trying to bite. But I had about thirty bites of my own. Together, we'd make a little dent in the population. The more we could take out on their way back up north, the fewer there would be for next year.

We'd have to come up with a more permanent solution someday. The sound system from Horizon would probably last at least a decade since we had pulled it all down and safely stored it in the caves. But no matter how many we managed to kill, the Flood would never stop. At least we had some time to figure it out.

A noise snapped me out of my vengeful rumination. It sounded like a strong wind, but deeper, and I couldn't place where it was coming from.

"You guys hear something?" I looked out across the valley and back behind me into the cave mouth, but saw nothing.

"I hear it," Josh said, and Shiro nodded.

"It's getting louder."

The deep rumble was joined by a higher pitched whine.

"Um . . . guys?" Shiro was looking straight up into the sky.

Through the distant fluffy clouds came the unmistakable silhouette of a spaceship.

It wasn't shaped like our little winged shuttles or our huge, ungainly transports. The ship was sleek and oblong, tapering to a point at what I assumed was the nose.

I turned to Josh. "Get everybody inside, now."

Shiro refused to move, and before Josh could start herding anyone into the caves, people started pouring out. In moments, half the population was crowded around the plateau, staring at the smooth silver ship descending slowly from the sky.

It gleamed in the light, reflecting the sun straight into my eyes. I stared until tears were running down my cheeks.

The people of Carthage were space travelers. We had come from a distant sun far across the galaxy to a planet that was full of alien life. We knew we weren't the only space-going species out there. But knowing you're not alone and seeing an alien craft landing in your sheep pasture were two very different things.

Mayor Borin had been moved back inside after the Flood, and was unable to come down in his wheelchair. I looked around the gathering, and almost everyone was shrinking back into the cave mouth. Nirah and Sara pushed forward to stand next to me and Shiro.

"So . . . what do we do?" Sara was looking at me. *Why does everyone always look at me?*

"I think . . . I think we go down and see what this is all about." There was no point in hiding. Anyone could tell from the gleaming state of the ship to the smooth, controlled landing that these space travelers were more advanced than us. If they wanted us dead, hiding in the caves was not going to help. Better to be a welcoming committee than a bunch of frightened shrews scurrying away.

The three of us marched down the hill and stood near the ship. Nothing on the slick surface indicated where a door might open, but there were some markings on the back end. They looked scratchily familiar.

Sara sucked in a breath. "See that? It says . . ."

She was cut off by a hissing noise. The side of the ship retracted and a long ramp slid out. We all backed up despite our brave intentions.

The first one out of the ship was a Birdman.

The second one out was my father.

I couldn't have stayed still if I tried. I rushed forward and threw myself into Dad's waiting arms. He was shaking and so was I, both of us clinging onto each other, standing on the ramp of the Birdman's ship.

When we finally pulled apart, I stared up into his face. "How did you . . .?"

Josh interrupted us, flinging himself into our hug.

The Birdman was watching silently just a few feet away. As

my family hugged and cried, four more Birdmen joined us, and Dad herded us down the ramp onto the ground.

I stared at them. We had seen their drawings and read their messages, left by the last of their colonists here. We even had the mummified remains of their archivist, reverently left where he had died, still clutching the paint that decorated our great hall. He was shriveled and dry, his brown feathers patchy and sparse.

Live Birdmen were magnificent. Three of them were brightly colored in patterns of blue and green. Their faces were beaky with bright black eyes. Their arms were covered in shimmering feathers, and ended in taloned fingers. The feathers looked like wings, but the only way these birds would fly was on a spaceship. No way the feathers would support their bodies, which were only a little shorter than me. The other two were feathered in shades of brown like the mummy in the cave, and I realized with a start that if they were like Earth birds, the brown ones were probably females. Which meant our mummified Birdman was actually a Birdwoman all along.

A squeal from the plateau drew my attention. With a delighted cry of "Birdman!" my sister Malia raced down the hill and across the field. Mom bolted after her but Malia was a streak of pale hair. She ran straight up to one of the brown ones and threw her little arms around the Birdwoman's legs, her little feet planted between the wicked sharp talons.

"Birdman!" she repeated.

Mom skidded to a halt just a few feet away. Nobody moved. *Those talons could rip a little girl apart in a heartbeat.*

The Birdwoman crouched down next to Malia, her feathered head cocking from side to side.

Malia reached into her pocket and pulled out her doll, the little Birdman toy Mom had made her. She thrust it into the Birdwoman's clawed hand and beamed up at the curved, sharp beak. "Look, it's you! My doll is you!"

The Birdwoman took the doll and turned it over, examining it carefully in her clawed fingers. She opened her beak and made a little chirping noise, and handed it back to Malia. With a gesture apparently common to mothers across the galaxy, she patted Malia on the head, chirped a little song, and gently ushered her back into Mom's waiting grasp.

And we all exhaled.

We sat in the sunshine and told our stories. Mayor Borin had been carried down, and the Birdpeople appeared fascinated by his wheelchair. They kept trying to lift up his pants to see what was wrong with his legs.

Dad and Mom sat with Malia between them. Josh held baby Teddy, whom Dad pronounced "perfect," and vowed to love as his own son. "We're all a family here. And now we've got some interesting new friends."

We were desperate to hear how he'd ended up on the Birdmen's ship, crazy to know what they were doing on a planet they'd abandoned decades before. But their chirping songs made no sense to Sara, who had disappeared into the caves with one of the females, no doubt heading for the Painted Hall. She'd be singing in their language in no time.

Dad told us his side of those last moments on Horizon.

"There was no way to get that arm off the shuttle. I had to do it manually from inside." His eyes were shining as he looked at Josh. "Closing that door, seeing your face through that window was the hardest thing I've ever done. And I knew I was a dead man. But it's funny how time slows down in those final moments.

"Horizon Alpha had escape pods."

My eyes widened at his words. "You ditched Horizon in an escape pod?"

He told us about his fall and crash into the ocean on the other side of the planet. "I just wanted to smell that fresh air once, feel the living planet under my feet. It was more than I could have ever imagined. The island I washed up on was tiny and desolate. No 'saurs, and no fresh water. I figured when the food and water from the pod ran out, that would be it for me."

Dad grinned at the Birdpeople, who had branched out and were now exploring our baby 'saur pen, tweeting excitedly at Ryenne who looked like a proud mama showing off her little pets. Ryenne's mom was standing at the gate with Rogan, who was rocking back and forth in excitement.

"They heard my pod's beacon."

Nirah looked puzzled. "How far did that beacon travel? Did they just happen to be passing by?"

Dad shrugged. "I don't think so, but I'm honestly not sure because I don't speak Birdman. But after they picked me up, which was quite a shock for all of us, they flew almost directly here. We went around by the mountains in the north, and I could see a couple of wrecked transports, but nobody alive. I was able to show them on their maps where you were, and we played space charades trying to get them to understand I wanted them to fly here. And here we are."

I looked at the smooth hull of the ship, and remembered the other times I had seen gleaming metal like that.

"Nirah, remember the pod in the mountains? You plugged in the numbers for pi and it started to flash?"

She nodded. "Of course. It was their own beacon. They must have left it when they abandoned this planet. Maybe thinking some other sentient species might someday come here. I wonder if they have them all over the galaxy?"

We marveled at the idea. How many worlds had these space travelers been to? Where were they going, and how would humans fit into their plans?

The sun was setting over the mountains and we harvested enough food for a feast. The Birdpeople were delighted with the fruit from the trees their ancestors had planted and left for us. They sniffed our dried meat and turned away, shaking their heads in presumed disgust. We gathered in the Painted Hall for the meal and the Birdpeople were obviously thrilled with the paintings left by their long-dead cousin. Sara was already working on a Birdpeople/English spoken dictionary, struggling to make the whistles and chirps with her new friend. The Birdwoman was attempting to croak out human words along with Sara, sounding a little like a scratchy parrot.

"It's a hard language for our mouths to make each others' sounds," she said around a mouthful of beet salad. "But it helps that I know the writing. Their ship, for example." She swallowed and took a long drink of water. "The markings on the tail are the ship's name. It means 'Fighting Bird.'"

That didn't sound promising, though they had shown no aggression in the hours we'd been escorting them around. "Like, Bird of Prey, you mean?" My younger, movie-loving self jumped up and down in my head, screaming excitedly in Klingon.

"Yeah, like that. 'Raptor,' maybe," Sara said.

Nirah and Sara were itching to get aboard the spaceship and check out the Birdpeople's technology. Everyone in the colony seemed to want to touch their shimmering feathers, which the Birdpeople didn't appear to mind. They were apparently fascinated by our hair, and reciprocated by pulling the women's long hair through their talons, chirping happily.

Mom held baby Teddy, and Dad held Malia on his lap. She didn't remember him, having left him on Horizon when she was just a baby, but we had raised her with stories of her father, and just like she accepted her new best friend the Birdwoman, she happily snuggled with this stranger we called "Dad." Josh and Shiro sat together across from me, and I looked at my family, complete and safe for the first time in three years.

My throat closed up as I gazed at each face. Mom had been my rock through every trial. Josh was my forever protector, the big brother who never believed in himself, but lived on my belief in him. Shiro, my almost-brother, the bravest soldier in Carthage. Dad, lost twice and found, weak and thin but beaming with joy. Baby Teddy, who had his biological father's eyes, blinking up at me with old wisdom and courage in the tiny round face. And Malia, who would be forever credited as first contact with a sentient alien race.

This was my family. This was my home. Whatever storms Tau Ceti could throw at us, we would weather them together. For the many lives lost in the pursuit of this moment of peace, I grieved. And for the generations to come, who would find their way in this strange and beautiful galaxy, I rejoiced.

We never would have come here if we'd known.

But in all the universe, there was nowhere else I would rather be than here with my family in a cave painted by bird aliens, on a planet full of dinosaurs.

The Wilde family was finally home.

ACKNOWLEDGEMENTS

The Horizon Alpha journey has brought me so many new experiences and opportunities. I'm forever grateful to everyone who's embraced Caleb and the 'saurs, and lived this adventure with me.

To my dedicated beta readers Nikolas Everhart and Jude Rose, thank you.

To my science advisor Joe Childers who keeps me just this side of plausible, thank you.

To my incredible agent Alice Speilburg, my champion, thank you.

To my editors Emma, Stephanie, and Isabelle, thank you.

To Adam, Emma, and all the amazing staff of Future House Publishing who first believed in the planet of dinosaurs, thank you.

To the fine folks of Cincinnati Fiction Writers, who twice a month put their souls on the line only to hear me say, "Are you sure that's where your story really starts?" thank you.

To my husband Andrew, who has learned which board games solo the best since his wife is upstairs typing away, thank you.

And to all my readers who have made this wonderful adventure possible, thank you, thank you, thank you.

ABOUT THE AUTHOR

D. W. Vogel is a veterinarian, marathon runner, cancer survivor, SCUBA diver, and current president of Cincinnati Fiction Writers. She is the author of the *Horizon Alpha* series from Future House Publishing, the fantasy novel *Flamewalker*, and the writing manual *Five Minutes to Success: Master the Craft of Writing*. She also has short stories in several anthologies from various publishers.

Wendy loves to hear from readers, so feel free to contact her on her website (https://wendyvogelbooks.com/) or on Twitter (https://twitter.com/drwendyv).

WANT D. W. VOGEL TO COME TO YOUR SCHOOL?

What makes a hero? Wendy has visited schools and museums to talk with kids about just that. Using Star Wars as an example, she takes a look at the classic Hero's Journey in literature. Ideal for grades 3–6, this is a fun introduction into the interpretation of story structure. Through the journey of Luke Skywalker, students will learn about courage and motivation, and the altruism that defines a real hero.

For more information visit: http://www.futurehousepublishing.com/authors/d-w-vogel/
Or contact: schools@futurehousepublishing.com